RIVER GOLD

The Civil War had toughened young Jerry Bryce but not stamped out the flame of humanity and justice which burned in his heart. What he found on the lonely Bakula River was like the war all over again with bitter hatred and anger festering alongside the greed for gold. There were innocent lives hanging in the balance and that thought alone dragged Jerry into a conflict he had no desire for.

BILL MORRISON

RIVER GOLD

Complete and Unabridged

LINFORD
Leicester

First published in Great Britain in 1998 by
Robert Hale Limited
London

First Linford Edition
published 1998
by arrangement with
Robert Hale Limited
London

British Library CIP Data

Morrison, Bill, *1931* –
River gold.—Large print ed.—
Linford western library
1. Western stories
2. Large type books
I. Title
823.9'14 [F]

LP

ISBN 0–7089–5381–6

Published by
F. A. Thorpe (Publishing) Ltd.
Anstey, Leicestershire
Set by Words & Graphics Ltd.
Anstey, Leicestershire
Printed and bound in Great Britain by
T. J. International Ltd., Padstow, Cornwall

This book is printed on acid-free paper

1

The heat hung heavy in the air, seeming to weigh down the flat landscape in fluid molten lead. The rain was on its way. He had seen it piling in massive clouds over the hills to the north-west and although he longed for its coolness, he knew that when it came, it would strike hard, for it had been a long time in coming and its energy had built up in all the weeks that he had spent on the long ride from Bluewater by way of the meandering valleys and the flats country.

Away ahead he could just make out the shimmering surface of the Bakula River. It was the first time in all his young life that he had seen it and, although it seemed an ordinary enough kind of river, this first glimpse gave him a start of surprise and nervous expectation which jolted through his mind so that he drew rein and sat silent for some minutes as if listening for a voice to echo across the emptiness.

Jerry Bryce felt very much alone. It was a feeling that had been with him for a long time, even before this journey had begun, before he got the strange letter, before the deaths of his parents even, although that sure enough, had rubbed in the feeling like salt in a wound.

He licked his dry lips and drew his sweaty, black hat a little further down over his straggling fair hair. His features, tanned by a life spent mostly in the open, already held lines of strain that conflicted with his air of youth.

He guessed the war had started it; the sensation of being empty and kind of lost. He had gone off to fight for the South as soon as he was old enough to enlist and had seen and felt the bloody conflict at first hand. He had watched his comrades die around him in that final Yankee charge which had left him unconscious. He had awakened much later in a night of dark rain to find his stumbling way through a field of corpses . . .

Soon after had come the surrender at Appomattox. He had made his slow way home to Bluewater with the conviction that it had all been in vain and with his heart sickened by the slaughter.

Even then it had not been over. The little farm lay neglected and almost derelict while his mother nursed her husband who had returned, some weeks earlier, with a bullet in his spine that no surgeon could get at. He had lain racked in pain until he was found one morning, empty eyes staring at the ceiling and his stiff fingers twisted into the blanket in some last agony.

Before he went, he had said a few things to Jerry, strange unsettling things, about his cousin, Mark Coney, and about being left in the lurch; face to face with the oncoming enemy when support should have been there. He described how the rest of the troops at the rear had melted away just when they were needed and how Coney had gone with them — Sergeant Coney vanishing with his own little squad of troopers, few in number, but essential at that precise moment as the Union soldiers advanced through the woods. It was then that Jeth Bryce had taken his wound and had lain helplessly as the fight rolled over him, back and forth. He had come to a day later in a Confederate field hospital with his body full of pain and his mind fixed upon the treachery of his cousin.

Jerry had listened intently to his father's ravings, trying to piece together the events surrounding that final skirmish and to discover what could have caused Coney to desert but it seemed clear that it could only have been an act of cowardice for which his father had paid with his mortal wound.

Even so, there was much left unexplained for Jeth Bryce and his cousin had been good friends in boyhood. They had gone off to war

4

as comrades in good cheer and with high hopes . . .

The thunder was rolling now over the hills, where the sky was darkening. Jerry turned to gaze in that direction while his mind lifted for a fleeting second from the memories which had hung upon him day after day on that long ride from the south. The Bakula was not so far away now. He could reach it probably by sundown. Then he must find a way over. Maybe there was a ford, though when that rain struck the river must rise, making such a passage more difficult or maybe impossible.

He rode on, urging his tiring horse, while the image of his mother's face as she lay dead floated once more before him. After the death of her husband she had gone in less than a week. Jerry had picked up the tools of farm labour to try to make some kind of success out of all the hardship and tragedy which had gone before.

How many months he had worked on

the farm on his own, he was uncertain. The time had gone by in a blur of heavy labour and exhausted sleep. Meals, he had snatched with little preparation and less thought. Then one day his mind jerked into sudden alertness as he pulled open a drawer in the parlour and found the letter, which had lain unread since his mother had placed it there at a time when nothing but her husband's fading life seemed of any importance to her.

Jerry had opened the letter in silent puzzlement. Even now, weeks later, he could remember the exact words without re-reading.

Jeth,

I am writing to ask you about the gold. Remember, that you picked up at Filey's Creek, just before the Yanks moved over? What did you do with it? Where did you hide it? We agreed to share everything! It isn't right that you don't let me in on it, after we got it together!

Write back and let me know that we're still buddies and are going to share — or come up here and see me. I am at a little homestead called Broken Rock just a few miles upstream from Bloomsferry on the Bakula River. For good reasons, I can't come to see you — one being that I got hit in the arm . . . But please write back or something. Do it quick!

Your cousin, Mark Coney.

There was no date. The writing was queer and lopsided as if it had been written with the left hand.

Jerry had pondered long and hard over that letter. It seemed to conflict with his father's last words. And what was this about gold? Jeth Bryce knew nothing of any gold — of that Jerry felt certain. And what was cousin Coney doing in this part of the country so long after the war was finished? All of this region had fought on the side of the Union, as Jerry had discovered as he rode, speaking from time to time with people who had reacted with faint hostility to his Southern accent. Coney had written something about a bad arm. Maybe that was the reason he had not returned to his home town; perhaps it was still pretty painful even after all this time.

Anyhow, he would not judge Mark Coney until they met again and he got the story out of him. Maybe he wasn't as much of a traitor as Jeth had thought.

Jerry believed in giving everybody a chance. He had seen too much of injustice and blind hatred in the mad conflict from which he himself had barely escaped with his life. He would listen to what Coney had to say and then he would decide if his sick father had spoken the truth, or had been too demented by pain to think straight.

But he knew also that if there was the need for action, if the mystery which lay somewhere up ahead called for the use of the gun which hung at his belt, then that's the way it would be. He had learnt that too in the war . . .

The rain was sweeping across the grasses by the late afternoon and the river, rising and turbulent, lay just ahead. Squinting against the wind-driven downpour, he could just make out a building and some kind of rough jetty on its near bank.

Bloomsferry! Pretty soon, he guessed, he would find out for sure.

2

The river was flowing swiftly and had
been stirred into roughness by the
mountain wind. Jerry stood upright
on the deck of the long ferryboat
that was nothing more than an old
barge attached by pulleys to the thick
rope that stretched from the posts on
one side of the river to those on the
other. He kept an anxious eye on his
nervous horse, tethered in the middle
of the boat, while he pulled with all
his might on the rope and pushed hard
with his feet. Behind him, the girl did
the same, but more expertly, and with
greater force in her legs and arms.

'I told ya it would be hard goin',
didn't I?' She smiled, showing a broken
tooth, while her black hair hung untidily
across her wet forehead. She was a hefty
girl, strong as most men, with a kind of
fat prettiness about her that struggled

to reveal itself through the ruddiness of her features.

'Maybe we should'a waited until the wind eased off, at any rate. I guess ya must be in a hell of a hurry ta git to wherever you're goin'. Ya wouldn't think, would ya,' she went on, 'thet I've got three big mule-headed brothers who could be out here helpin' if they wasn't still lyin' in bed drunk, where they've been fer the last couple of days! Seem ta think that I kin do all the work. not thet I mind helpin' a young feller like you.' She glanced at him with a little hint of admiring interest.

'But I wouldn't do this jest fer anybody, no sir! I generally tie up the boat when the river's like this an' cook myself a decent meal, since there ain't anybody else ta do it fer me. I'm having chicken tonight. Ya like chicken? If ya wasn't in such a hurry, ya could stay an' have some. Give me somebody to talk to besides a passel o' drunks . . . '

Jerry shook his head and took one hand off the rope for a second to signal that he appreciated the offer but must decline it due to a pressing engagement. He was too much out of breath to talk.

'Where did ya say you was goin'?'

'Broken Rock.'

His reply was lost in the wind and she made no further attempt to converse until they had hauled themselves all the way over the river and had reached the little jetty on the other bank. There, they managed, after several attempts, to coax the horse over the planks and on to the dry land. Glad to get safely ashore, he grinned and paid her twice the normal fare for the trip, which was what she had insisted upon before setting off on such a difficult journey.

'Did ya say Broken Rock?'

'Yeah. Do ya know it?'

'Sure. It's jest a little place up thataway. Wouldn't have thought a feller like you would be goin' there. Ain't nothin'ta see.'

'I'm looking fer somebody — Mark Coney. Ya heard tell of him?'

'Coney? Don't know about that. Couple o' fellers stay there, sure enough. Old kind of fellers — older than you by a long ways, anyhow. Southerners, I heard tell.' She looked at him, eyes suddenly suspicious.

'You're a Southerner, ain't ya?' She leaned towards him, the suspicion going for a second to be replaced by teasing flirtation. 'I kin tell by your accent. Ya sound jest as if ya come from the south and you've got it written all over ya. Not that I mind. Some Southerners are all right, in spite of bein' lousy Rebs!' She laughed and put a hand on his shoulder. 'Sure ya don't want to stay fer dinner?'

'Sorry. It's real good of ya but I gotta git on my way.'

'Mark Coney, huh?' She was looking more thoughtful as if she were ransacking her memory. 'I'm sure I've heard of somebody with a name like thet . . . but I tell ya, there ain't nobody at Broken

Rock except two old fellers, names of Smith an' Brown. Thet's it. Thet's what I heard. Jest them an' the Chinee gal. Ain't never seen them at all. They never come down thisaway. Seen the Chinee gal, though, sometimes. She rides inta McCarry Ridge fer supplies every now and agin.'

'Chinese gal?'

'Yeah. She seems like a kind of servant there. Does the cookin' an' stuff. I don't know what else she does fer these two old fellers!' She raised her eyebrows archly. 'Who knows? Never kin tell, especially with them foreigners!' Her grin spread, broad and knowing. 'Hope ya ain't come all this way jest ta meet her, you devil you! She's pretty, mind you, I got to admit it. In a Chinee way, of course!'

Jerry grinned back, covering his irritation.

'No, no, nothin' like thet. But see here, I got to git goin'. Thanks fer everythin'. S'long!'

'Be seein' ya.' She let him go with

regret. 'Remember ta drop in agin next time ya pass by. Hey, my name's Judy! What's yours?'

'Jerry — Jerry Bryce.'

He rode on, glad to get away and was soon busy again with his thoughts. What he had heard from the ferry-girl did not sound encouraging and he wondered if he had delayed too long. Perhaps Mark Coney had left Broken Rock for some reason and these two other men had taken the place over. Somehow, though, he did not think that was the case. The girl had spoken as if Smith and Brown had lived there for a long time.

The track that led up the east side of the river was narrow and little used but easy enough to follow. The rain had eased off but the wind was still in his face. Once he looked back and saw the boat half way back across the stream while Judy hauled manfully at the rope. The daylight was beginning to fade and he saw an oil-lamp appear in one of the rough buildings on the bank towards which she was heading. The low building near the jetty on the east side remained in darkness. For the first time since leaving the farm, he felt really alone and for a moment he almost regretted the impulse which had set him on his present course.

He put the idea out of his head but, at the same time, made up his mind that he could not make much more progress that day. He was tired and so was his horse, and he felt, somehow, that he might need all his wits about him when he got to Broken Rock. For those reasons, he forced himself to halt, to ground-tether his mount, and to settle down to sleep with his saddle as a pillow and his rough blanket wrapped around his body.

He awoke with the sun in his face and the feeling that he was being watched. For a moment, he did not open his eyes. He knew that there was a horse standing nearby which was not his own. He could hear its breathing and the faint rattle of the bit in its mouth. He thought about his gun, fear creeping through the hair at the back of his neck, but reckoned that to reach for it in its place under the saddle would probably be a serious mistake.

Slowly, he forced his eyelids apart, just enough to squint against the sunlight which streamed from the east.

As he had felt, a figure loomed against the sky, on horseback, partly silhouetted in the morning light and with a stillness which suggested that he had been under observation for some time.

Cautiously, he pushed himself up on his elbows, nerving himself for the bullet or the blow that had hung over his mind as he groped into consciousness. But the figure did not move and, raising his hand to shade his eyes from the sun, he saw to his surprise and relief that it was a girl.

'The Chinee gal'. Judy's description flitted back into his mind, and he raised himself a little further to look at her. She was dressed in a buckskin jacket over a white shirt with fringed trousers and neat little riding boots. On the back of her head was a stetson, its blackness matching that of her hair. Her eyes, dark, almond-shaped, gazed down at him with a coolness that hinted at disdain. Her fingers were small and dainty but lingered over the butt of the pistol which she carried on her hip.

Abruptly, he pushed himself to his feet, anxious to get up from his position of disadvantage, his hands brushing some of the dirt and grass from his pants as if he felt that he ought to tidy himself up for such company.

She did not move as he gazed at her for a long moment. God, he thought, but she's pretty! The ferry girl had been right about that. She was beautiful with a glowing freshness about her like flowers coming into bloom and with a serenity in her features such as he had never seen before. At last, she smiled and her face lit up in a way that almost made him gasp.

'I am sorry. I did not mean to disturb you but I saw your horse and wondered who was here.'

Her voice sounded like that of a bird singing in the forest. He cleared his throat with difficulty.

'It's okay, ma'am. I must have overslept anyway.'

'You are looking for somewhere? We do not get many people here, that is why I ask. Perhaps I can direct you?'

'Yeah, well, the thing is, maybe you can. I'm aimin' to git to a place called Broken Rock.'

If she was surprised she did not show it in her face although she hesitated before replying.

'Why do you wish to go there?'

'I want to see a man named Mark Coney. He there?'

'What makes you think I should know?'

'Well, thing is, the gal at the ferry said that you and a couple of — of gentlemen live there. She said . . . '

'She said about me?'

'Well, she mentioned the — the Chinese gal. I hope ya . . . '

'She is a donkey. I am of Nippon — Japanese. This Mr Coney — do you have business with him?'

'I got a letter.' He watched her eyes widen just a little as he explained the circumstances. 'By the way, miss, my name's Jerry Bryce.'

'My name is Fasuko,' she said quietly. She looked at him as if measuring him up, as if estimating how much confidence she might have in him. 'I and my father have lived in Broken Rock for a lot of years, since I was a child. My parents were servants of the people who used to own the farm. Then the war came and they went away to join the South but they did not want us so we just stayed. There did not seem anywhere to go. Then my mother died.'

'I am sorry to hear thet.' He was, he had to admit to himself, fascinated by

20

her. For the moment, it seemed that he just wanted to stand there, gazing at her and listening to her talk in that lilting songbird accent.

'It's all right, Mr Bryce, we all have our sorrows in this world — you as well as me.' She smiled as if there was already a bond between them. 'There is no escape from sorrow.'

He remained silent, suddenly thrown into embarrassment. She continued to look down at him in the same calm, placid way. Then she said, 'Mr Coney is dead also. I am sorry.'

'Oh, what? But the letter?'

'Perhaps it was sent a long time ago? It must have been for he has been dead for' she made a vague gesture with her delicate hands 'a long time. Was there a date on it?'

'Well, no, but I thought . . . '

'The war — everything fell into confusion. The mail has been bad like all things.'

'You knew my uncle? How did he die?'

21

'The war too . . . ' She fell silent once more as if thinking out her response. 'He was wounded. He died up there at Broken Rock.' Then she smiled at him kindly. 'Come with me to the house. You can meet Mr Brown and Mr Smith. They may be able to help you to sort out what is in your mind. They were friends of Mr Coney. Also, you can be our guest for as long as you wish.'

She turned her horse and began to move up the slight rise. For the first time, he noticed a mule standing some yards away, heavily laden. Seeing him glance she explained, 'I have been to McCarry for supplies. I camped out last night, then I saw your horse in the morning.'

She waited patiently while he saddled up and then she led the way along the narrow track beside the river. She rode a short distance ahead and made no attempt at further conversation. It was as if she felt that she must not inquire into his business and that Mr Brown and Mr Smith could explain whatever had to be explained better than she.

At length the buildings of Broken Rock came into sight. They consisted of a small farmhouse of mixed stone and timber and some wooden outbuildings. Just beyond, he could make out the surface of the river itself and a jetty with some kind of boat tied up to it. As they drew nearer, he saw that the whole place was pretty run-down. The fields were a mass of weeds and much of the fencing was in need of repair. Two horses and another mule in a corral towards the rear of the house lifted their heads at the sound of hooves. A few goats and chickens wandered at will. Messrs Brown and Smith, thought Jerry, whatever else the men were, could not call themselves farmers.

When they reached the front of the house, Fasuko dismounted, hitched her horse to a post, did the same for the mule, and then signalled for Jerry to tie up his horse.

'Do not worry about them too

much,' she remarked. 'Do not become angry. They will not mean any harm to you.'

He gaped at her in astonishment, wondering what she meant, but followed her in silence up the path to the sun-bleached front door. They had almost reached it when the shutters of a nearby window flew open and the barrel of a rifle appeared, pointing straight at Jerry.

'Halt right there, stranger!' The voice was thick, throaty and full of menace. 'One more step an' yo're dog meat!'

Jerry suddenly froze. Fasuko continued up to the wooden steps as if she had not heard. She undid her gunbelt and hung up her pistol on a hook by the porch. Then she turned to him, smiling. For the first time, he noticed how small she was, hardly more than five feet, but as elegant as an antelope.

'Drop that gun! Right now, stranger!' The voice from the window was more threatening than ever. 'I've got ya covered real good!'

Irritation rose high in Jerry's throat but Fasuko was holding out her hand, inviting him to do what was asked. Reluctantly, he took off the belt and handed it to her. She hung it beside her own and then led the way into the house.

The room seemed almost bare with only a rough wooden table, a few chairs and an iron stove. An old clock and a Bible stood on a shelf to one side. Apart from a remnant of rug on the floorboards, there was nothing else. The sense of poverty was almost tangible in the air.

The man at the window had turned from the swinging shutters and crouched against the sill, gun still pointing in Jerry's direction. He was small, bent and grey-haired. His sharp little nose seemed to sniff for a sign of danger like a polecat. Small, beady eyes stared intently, narrowed now to tiny points of suspicion. At the table sprawled a much bigger man, flabby-jawed and balding. He was still gripping a tin mug of coffee, which dripped on to the table top as he tilted it over in his surprise.

'Who the hell's this?' breathed the man at the window. 'What does he want? Where's he from?'

'Put the gun away, Casey,' suggested Fasuko, calmly. 'This is Mr Jerry Bryce. He has . . . '

'Casey? What the hell you mean, Casey?'

'Sorry, Mr Brown. Put the gun away, Mr Brown, and this — eh — gentleman, the one having breakfast, this is Mr Smith.'

The man at the table grunted and then clattered his mug on to the table. 'Did ya git the beer an' whiskey?'

'I got a little beer but no whiskey. Whiskey is expensive and it is not what you should drink. I got food which is what we require.'

'Listen, Jappo, when I say to git whiskey, that's what I mean! How the hell cain't ya git what I ask fer?'

'Do not call me Jappo unless you

wish to go in to McCarry to buy your own stores. Do you understand that, Flynn?'

'Christ!' The fat man looked aghast, glancing at Jerry in horror. 'Take it easy. Who the hell's this? How do ya know who this guy is? I'm Smith.' He nodded to Jerry as if in a belated but polite attempt to introduce himself. 'Gal gits mixed up sometimes,' he explained weakly.

Jerry stood silently, trying to take in the situation. It stuck in his nostrils like a bad smell. The idea of this fine girl living under the same roof as these dead-beats struck him to the heart. His heart tightened as he fought down a growing sense of outrage.

'Mr Bryce came all the way in the hope of meeting his cousin, Mark Coney.'

Fasuko made the announcement and then remained quiet as if to observe the effect. Both men opened their eyes wide in astonishment. Casey looked alarmed and reached again for his guns; Flynn's eyes rolled and a hunted expression swept across his face. Neither spoke for a short space of time and then Flynn shrugged his massive shoulders as the fear went from his features to be replaced by exaggerated unconcern.

'Well,' he grinned wetly, showing bad teeth as the joke came out flat and humourless. 'He kin find his cousin around the back of the paddock. If he wants to see him, he'd better take the spade!'

Jerry made no attempt to hide the contempt he felt. 'Your manners,' he remarked bitterly, 'are lousy.'

Tension rose in the room. The two men stared at him with undisguised hostility. Casey raised the barrel of the rifle a fraction but lowered it as he met something cold and determined in Fasuko's eyes.

'Mr Bryce received a letter which was addressed to his father. It was from Coney so Mr Bryce decided to come here.' She turned her gaze from one to the other, a hint of a smile touching her lips. 'I understand that Mr Bryce — that is, Jerry's father — and Mark Coney, his cousin, were in the army together. Is that not interesting? But Jerry's father died of a war wound and, of course, so did Mark Coney. Anyway, Jerry is now here and he should be treated as an honoured guest. Please sit down, Jerry, and I will make fresh coffee.'

Her words seemed to take some of the heat out of the situation, at least for a few seconds, then Flynn stared anew at Jerry and screwed his mouth up as if to bring out words which stuck in his throat.

'Yer pa,' he asked, grimly, 'where did he git hit? Where was it?'

'Filey's Creek,' answered Jerry at once.

They both stared, eyes wide with apprehension.

'Jesus,' whispered Casey.

3

The grave was just flat earth, hard-packed pebble-strewn mud, drying out after the rain of the day before. There was no headstone, not as much as a rough wooden cross. Jerry stood looking at it dully, Fasuko by his side. He felt nothing but a resentment that nothing more than this had been done. There was no sense of grief as cousin Coney had meant little to him. Nevertheless he felt any man's grave, whoever he was or whatever he might have done, should look like something better than the corner of a neglected yard.

They were silent for some minutes, Fasuko seeming to guess at his thoughts. They were both acutely aware also of being under observation from the two grey-clad figures who stood at the window of the farmhouse. Brown and Smith — Casey and Flynn — had not let him out of sight since his arrival and had seemed reluctant to allow him this much space, or this semblance of privacy, even for a little while.

'Fasuko,' Jerry's voice was as low as he could pitch it. 'What really happened to Coney? Kin ya tell me?'

'He came here one day, badly wounded,' she whispered, 'as if he had been in a battle. He seemed to expect to see the people who had the farm before the war. He said that he knew them. He lingered for a few days, then the other two arrived as if they had been following his tracks or maybe he had told them where he was going. Anyway, they came but he died a day later.'

'What's goin' on here? I don't get it. Why do they stay?'

'They need me. They are afraid to leave so I am the only person who can bring them in supplies. Without me, they starve or venture out to face what they are afraid of.'

'Why don't ya git out, though? Why come back?'

'My father is here. If I do not return or if I betray them, he will be the first to suffer.'

Jerry had seen her father, an old bent Japanese who spent all his time in the kitchen.

'Dirty scum . . . ' He struggled to control the anger rising up in his mind. 'I knew it was somethin' like that. What about the law — the sheriff from McCarry, maybe? Have ya not told anybody?'

'No. It would be the same. There would be a fight but my father would be dead before it started.'

'But all this time! Since the war! How kin ya go on? Ain't ya scared?'

'Yes, but I pretend not to be.'

'Yeah, I know, but a young gal like you, with them two polecats . . . ' His voice trailed off in anger.

She was quiet for a moment and when she replied her voice was like finely sharpened steel cutting the air above the grave. 'If they attempt to harm me they will not sleep any night for fear of a knife at their throats. Also, even if I failed in that, I would kill myself and then they would be lost. They know that. They need me alive and prepared to help them. Without me, they cannot stay here.'

He knew that she meant every word and that they must have known it too. Whenever she spoke, it was with a certainty that did not allow for argument.

'These two fellers, though.' He jerked his head slightly back towards the window and then felt like kicking himself for his mistake. 'What are they scared of? Why don't they git t'hell outa here? They could maybe git away some time in the dark — at night. They cain't stay here forever!'

'There was some sort of crime. Something about stolen gold. They asked Coney where he had put the gold but he was too ill to say — or he did not want to. After he died, they were very suspicious of each other. Each thought that the other might have picked up some clue from Coney and would find and keep the gold for himself. They argued all the time — sometimes fought with their fists. After that, they just watched one another like hawks and watched me too because they thought I might know something. They threatened me and my father but I told them what would happen if they did us harm and they were beginning to realize that they were going to need me so they made me swear on the Bible that I knew nothing.'

Gold! So there *was* gold! Coney had written about it in his letter to Jeth Bryce. Jerry stared harder than ever at the ground, wondering whether his own father had been mixed up in it, but he dismissed the thought as soon as it came into his mind. Jeth Bryce had always been strictly honest in all his dealings. He turned and looked at Fasuko, unable for the moment to see her face as she bent her head towards the grave. He had not told her that Coney had mentioned gold in the letter, which still lay crumpled in his pocket.

'Hey!' Casey came scuffling up behind them, dragging his rifle, still suspicious and irritated. 'What are ya two jawin' about? No sense in standin' around here all day! Ain't gonna make ol' Coney git up an' outa there, is it? Come back inside. Me an' my buddy, Smith, want to talk some more to you.'

He lifted the rifle in partial threat. Jerry felt like striking him regardless of the likelihood of taking a bullet. What Fasuko had just told him filled him with anger and he felt that he wanted to bring matters to a head at once because he knew it could not go on much longer. He must do something about these vermin who had latched themselves on to the lives of this gentle girl and her harmless old father! But what could he do? He had allowed himself to be disarmed and his gun had been taken down from the hook in the porch along with that of Fasuko, who was only permitted to carry a weapon for her own protection when she was away from the house.

He followed Casey back to the house, aware that Flynn now stood at the window with rifle at the ready. The faded grey clothing they both wore was now recognizable to him as the remnants of uniforms of the Southern military, stripped of every brass badge and button.

He sat at the table reluctantly, curbing his temper. Already they had asked him every question they could think of without mentioning the magic word 'gold'. He had given them the facts as he knew them but not revealed the contents of the letter beyond saying that Coney had informed his cousin, Jeth Bryce, that he was at Broken Rock.

'This here letter,' Flynn growled,

picking at his nose. 'When did ya say ya got it?'

'Don't rightly know. Months ago, anyhow.'

'Coney died a helluva long time ago. Couldn't have sent it after he was dead, could he?'

'You're a real smart bastard managing to figure thet out,' replied Jerry.

Flynn swung his fist but the width of the table prevented it from connecting.

'Okay, take it easy,' intervened Casey. 'We don't want to kill his pig's bladder jest yet. Maybe later. I reckon he knows more than he makes out. We'll git it outa him yet. Listen, yeller-belly, what we want to know is how ol' Coney could have sent it. Gal says she didn't take it down to Bloomsferry for the mail afore we got here, so how could he say he was at Broken Rock?'

'Don't ask me. I jest got it. I didn't send it.'

'Mebbe he jest sent it off when he was ridin' past some mail station on his way up here — if he knew where he was goin',' put in Flynn.

'Course he knew. He told us didn't he? Says about them folks. Helluva risky thing to do though, weren't it? Must've reckoned it was real important to tell his cousin where he was headed. He might have been picked up easy while he was mailin' it! He wasn't all thet much further ahead than we . . . '

'Shaddup!' growled Flynn.

They were silent for some minutes then Flynn stared at Jerry. His eyes were dull but held, nevertheless, an angry suspicious gleam.

'You said yer pa got hit at Filey's Creek. Thet the time the Yanks came over an' then got driven back not all thet long afore Lee reckoned the South was licked?'

'My father was wounded not long before Lee surrendered.' Jerry found it hard to make the statement without a slight tremble coming into his voice. 'After thet, he came home and died.'

'Why the blazes would Coney write

a letter to his cousin in — what's the name of the place? — Bluewater, if his cousin was still at Filey's Creek?'

'Don't tell this jerk too much,' put in Casey.

'It don't much matter now,' grunted Flynn. 'He knows more than he's gonna walk out of here with as it is.'

'You will not do him harm,' said Fasuko from her place by the door.

'Shut your trap!' snapped Casey. 'Seems to me you've had too much to say fer yourself lately.'

'You said it,' agreed Flynn. 'Anyway, what's your interest in this feller? You gettin' sweet on him?' He laughed without humour. 'Thought it was jest your ol' man thet ya was lookin' out fer?'

Fasuko did not reply. Casey had pulled a pistol from his belt and held it now, arm steadied on the table, pointing at Jerry's stomach.

'Let's see the letter,' he hissed.

Jerry shook his head, hiding a sudden

surge of fear. 'I guess not,' he replied firmly, conscious that he was learning something from Fasuko. 'It's my letter. Nobody reads it without my say-so.'

'Maybe ye'd rather take a bullet in the guts an' we kin read the goddamned letter after!'

'Won't do ya any good to shoot me. Ya could be missin' out on somethin'.'

The bluff seemed to be working. Both men looked uncertain. They stared at one another, nonplussed. Then Flynn spread his wet lips into a semblance of a smile and adopted a tone of voice that was intended to appeal to reason and commonsense.

'OK, so you reckon ya know something thet we don't, but I bet we know a helluva lot thet you don't. Right? You was never at Filey's Creek, so ya don't know what happened. Sometimes when fellers work together they kin git things worked out so as to suit them all. Ya git the idea?'

'You say ya came all the way up

40

here to see Coney — thet right?' put in Casey. 'Why did ya want to speak to him?'

'He was my cousin. I hadn't seen him since the start of the war. Why wouldn't I want to see my own cousin?' Jerry's answer was less than convincing, as he intended it to be. An idea was beginning to evolve in his mind. It held untold risk for himself but it might save Fasuko and that, he suddenly knew, was more important than anything for him.

'There ain't no use in lyin',' snarled Casey.

'Ya cain't kid us!' agreed Flynn.

They watched him closely, waiting upon a response but he remained tight-lipped, like a man with much that he could tell but with no intention of telling it.

'What did Coney tell ya about the gold?' asked Casey.

'Christ! Do ya think . . . ?' objected Flynn.

'It don't matter. We cain't keep

pussy-footin' around for ever. What did Coney tell ya?'

'Coney didn't tell me anythin'. He wrote to my father.'

The butt of the gun rapped on the table.

'Don't git smart, yeller-belly, my trigger finger's itchin' like hell!'

'Seems to me he spoke to yer father as well since they was both at Filey's Creek around the same time,' suggested Flynn.

'Could be,' answered Jerry calmly.

There came a faint sound from somewhere outside at the front of the house. It could have been the jingle of a bit chain, half smothered by the window shutters closed to keep out the afternoon sun. All suddenly fell silent. Casey and Flynn stared fixedly. Flynn seemed to pale through the gnarled ruddiness of his complexion. Casey's finger whitened on the trigger so that Jerry tensed in expectation of the promised bullet.

'Anybody at home?' the voice sang

42

out, male and youthful.

Nobody in the room moved. A fly buzzed noisily around near the ceiling.

'Anybody there? Mr Coney there?'

Flynn breathed in sharply. Casey swung round, gun turned towards the window.

'Mr Coney? Mark Coney?'

Casey jerked a hand, motioning Fasuko to go to the door. She did so, opening it wide so that her trim figure stood silhouetted against the sudden square of sunlight. The horse sounds increased, a hoof thudding in the dirt, the snorting of laboured breath, but to the practised ears of those in the room, there was only one horseman outside — no more.

'Hey, the Chinee gal!' The voice was raised higher in pretended delight, pleasant enough still but with the hint of a jeer lingering in its wake. 'Say, missee, you got Mr Coney livin' here?'

'Mr Coney does not live here,' answered Fasuko with truth.

43

'Yeah? Well you got anybody else? Southern gentlemen, maybe?'

Flynn and Casey rose from the table, guns in fists. Floorboards creaked viciously as they attempted a silent crossing to the windows. Casey drew back the shutter, letting in a shaft of light. From his seat at the table, Jerry craned to see and made out the head and shoulders of a black-haired youth of about seventeen, pimply faced but smooth cheeked. He was grinning towards Fasuko at the door but turned his head at the sound of the opening shutter.

'Hey, there's somebody there sure enough missee! Who's thet? Ain't Mr Casey?'

Both guns exploded as one. The youth jerked violently in the saddle and screamed. It was high-pitched, childish, almost like that of a girl. He toppled from Jerry's view but the sound of his body thudding into the hardening mud of the yard seemed to reverberate into the room. Bucking and neighing told of his horse swinging round to bolt.

'Git the horse!' yelled Casey. 'Git it!'

Fasuko ran from the doorway.

4

They stood in silence around the body of the youth, hushed into quiet by the sudden tragedy or thrown into shock by the unforeseen emergency. For minutes they stared without speech at his outstretched form, lean and supple, but with one arm reached out now in a frantic last gesture to hold on to the short life which had abruptly slid from him. His eyes were wide open, staring like their own, but taking on the cold of death. His mouth was partially open and full of blood.

Fasuko leaned with her trembling hands on the post to which she had hitched his frightened mount. She had moved with speed to seize it and control it and now gazed at the dead boy with her face an oriental mask of grief.

Jerry felt numb. A confused jumble of

thoughts and emotions strove to make sense of what lay before him. Horror and anger struggled for expression.

'You rats . . . ya dirty, low . . . '

Casey's Colt .45 came up. His hand shivered.

'Shut yer mouth, Bryce, or you'll git it too.'

There was a razor edge of tension. One further word, another hint of anger or opposition, the slightest movement of outraged protest, and those guns would sound again in frantic unison and he must sprawl in the dirt with his life jumping out of his useless rage.

He waited and waited, seeming to wait in the shadow of the kid's death. At length, Flynn spoke in a voice that, at first, scarcely seemed his own.

'He knew about us. He said Coney an' Casey. How did he know them names?' He lifted his head and shifted it around the little group with the slow surliness of an ill-tempered bear. 'Bryce? You say somethin' to them

47

folks at the ferry? Ya musta' said somethin'.'

Jerry licked his lips, trying to control his mouth and his mind.

'I said to the girl thet I was lookin' for Coney, thet's all . . . '

'Ya say anythin' about Casey?'

'I never heard of goddamned Casey!'

The bullet from Casey's gun came angry, jittery and badly aimed. It tore a strip of cloth from Jerry's shirt sleeve alongside skin and a spattering of blood. Jerry clapped his hand to the burning pain.

'Ya didn't make some kinda plan with anybody?'

'What kinda plan would it be,' growled Jerry through his teeth, 'to send this kid up here to git shot?' He had been about to use the word 'murdered' but thought better of it.

'Who is this kid, anyhow?' Flynn turned to Fasuko. 'You know most of the folks around here. Least you've seen them around. He from the ferry?'

'No, he does not live there but he's

related to them. I think he comes from a family over at Humblestream Ford.'

'What kinda place is thet — this Humblestream?'

'Just a farm. Bigger than this, better than this. The family is called Galbraith. They are cousins to those at the ferry.'

'So there's been talk. Folks gabbin' an' rememberin' an' fittin' things up together.' Flynn was nodding his fat head at Casey as if he had come up with an idea that nobody else could have thought of. 'This kid had heard somethin' about it and came up here, nosin' around, maybe not knowin' what he was gittin' himself into.'

'He'll be missed afore long,' grunted Casey morosely, 'an' then they'll be up here searchin', even if they don't know already where he is.'

Flynn jerked his gun. There was a look in his eye which brooked no argument. He was a man getting towards the end of his rope.

'You two — git into the kitchen with the old man. Don't try nothin'. Me an' Casey's got some figuring to do.'

Fasuko and Jerry walked slowly into the house. Both still felt as if they had suffered a terrible personal injury by witnessing the murder of the boy. All Fasuko's confidence and control seemed to have waned. She still trembled and bit her lip to hold back tears. She no longer seemed capable of standing up to these men as she had done before. Everything had changed. No longer was there a balance of power in this shabby household. There were just the guns and a sense of urgency and a need to bring matters to an end.

Inside the dim kitchen, her father bent over the stove, stirring a pot. He looked up as they entered and smiled thinly at Jerry. His wrinkled features seemed calm but his tiny eyes held a hint of anxiety. He had heard the shots but had not ventured out to investigate. Jerry nodded to him, too grim within himself to smile. The old man put down the spoon and lifted a small brass figure of a Buddha from the shelf near the window. He polished it carefully with a piece of rag, almost as if he were alone.

'Fasuko,' Jerry's voice was tense but low and controlled, 'if you and your father were left alone here — if I rode away with these scum — could you leave? Would ya git out of it? Git clear away?'

She looked at him steadfastly, her own fear and shock now held in check.

'Yes, we would go at once. It is what I have dreamed of. We would go by the river. There has never been any chance before.'

Jerry remembered the boat at the river's edge and nodded. The idea in his mind, he went to the window to look towards the river bank and started as he saw Casey lead a horse in that direction. It was the young feller's horse, a fine animal, young and strong. Man and horse vanished down the bank and a moment later another shot rang out. Casey reappeared, thrusting his gun back into its holster.

'Dirty scum!' Jerry felt anger raging through his heart. Casey was getting rid of the evidence, fearful that it might be seen by anyone out searching for the boy. 'Listen, Fasuko.' He turned to face her again. 'I'm goin' to make out that I'm throwin' myself in with them two snakes so as to lead them away from here. I think I kin do it!' He nodded grimly. 'I want you to git on your way as soon as we're out of sight, jest in case they change their minds. You'll do thet?'

'Yes, we'll travel well away from here.'

He gazed at her with mixed feelings, glad to hear her promise to save herself but suddenly despairing at the thought of never seeing her again.

'Where could ya go?' He had not meant to ask the question but it had come out unbidden for this seemed too final a break and he needed some promise of a lifeline between them, however tenuous.

'We would go to Higson-Bar. It is a town a long way downriver.' She smiled faintly, seeming to read his thoughts. 'It is on the west bank of the river. It is easy for a person to find.'

For a second he felt a light uplifting of his spirits. It was as if she cared a little for him. Jesus, he had only just met her, but somehow it was as if she had become all important in his life! He grinned with a hint of embarrassment and then turned for the door. He pushed it open and strode into the front room.

'Hey!' Flynn was on his feet, big mouth gaping in protest. 'We told ya to stay in there till we was through speakin'!'

'Okay, but I've got somethin' to say to you. You'd better jest sit back and listen if ya want to git anythin' outa all this except bullets or a hangin'. I got a proposition.'

Casey had come back into the house and caught the words. They stared at one another and then Jerry sat down at the table without invitation and glared at Flynn. He then rummaged in his pockets and drew out Coney's letter, which he smoothed. 'I'm gonna read you this.' Flynn's mouth twisted as if to say that he had intended reading it anyway just as soon as they had used up another bullet but he said nothing as Jerry read the contents.

When he had finished, Jerry looked up at them, seeing their eyes widen and harden at the mention of the gold.

'So ya see, Coney and my father were in cahoots about the gold.'

'Yeah, maybe thet double-crossing skunk did pass it on somehow to Trooper Bryce,' Flynn was staring unblinkingly as if to penetrate into Jerry's brain. 'But it don't say nothin' about where the stuff is, does it?'

'How could he have passed it to Bryce?' protested Casey. 'We was . . . '

'There was all thet shootin' remember?

Dempsey an' Cindy got killed. We was all separated in the dark. Maybe there was some other fellers in it too, thet we didn't know about — like this here Bryce.'

'Yeah, my father spoke of Dempsey and Cindy as well as Coney,' put in Jerry, lying his way further into the gamble. 'Then he told me where it was hidden — he gave me a pretty good idea, anyhow. I would know the exact place if I got to it. That's why I came up here. I knew thet my cousin would know how to git to Filey's Creek and I reckoned it was only right thet we should share.'

'Share what?' asked Casey, mouth twisting.

'The gold.'

'What kinda' gold? What are ya talkin' about exactly?'

Jerry felt his feet on the edge of a swamp that could drown him. He had only read the word 'gold'. He had never known in what form the gold might be. There were plenty of possibilities — gold ingots, gold dust, nuggets, coins, gold plate, jewellery. He had thought about it, but had come to no conclusion. A wrong guess here could kill him — would kill him — so it was safer to admit ignorance.

'I don't rightly know. My father was dying. Sometimes he spoke clearly, other times he was real confused and only said things in halves. It wasn't easy to understand everything he meant.'

'So what makes ya think he told ya right where the stuff's hid?' Casey was leaning forward, sneeering out his suspicion.

'He said that bit pretty clear,' answered Jerry looking him straight in the eye.

He knew that they had nothing better to go on. If they had any clue at all as to the where-abouts of the gold, they would have got to it by now, regardless of the risk of being recognized as outlaws or thieving deserters or whatever they felt they were. Fasuko had said that

56

they spent days searching around the farm to find out if Coney had hidden it just before his death. After that, they had not known what else to do except suspect one another and watch every movement in case Casey knew more than Flynn or Flynn knew more than Casey. At the same time they had kept their heads down and used her as their only go-between with the outside world. They had almost been in a state of paralysis since they had come to realize that the gold had vanished. Now everything had changed. His own arrival had forced them to think afresh; the dead boy still lying out in the yard told them that they had better make a move before others did.

'So what's this helluva proposition?' Flynn slouched forward, looking sarcastic, saliva dripping from his mouth on to the table.

'You lead me to Filey's Creek. I pick out the place where the stuff is. We share it fifty-fifty . . . fifty to me an' . . . '

'You got to be kiddin',' growled Casey. 'Three ways or nothin'.'

Something like an ironic laugh swelled into Jerry's chest. Casey was rising to the bait.

'Well, I don't know about thet. After all, without me, ya won't find the stuff.'

'I got a better proposition,' grunted Flynn. 'You tell us right now everythin' ya know or we drill yer guts.'

'Kill me and nobody gits anythin',' answered Jerry with outward calm. He believed himself to be on fairly safe ground. They were recognizing that he was their only chance. They would obviously do better to ride out with him and a promise of the gold rather than to ride away with nothing. Sure, they intended killing him as soon as the gold was in their hands. That he had known from the start of the plan coming into his mind. There was no other way with men like them, but he would face that when he had to. What he needed was time — time for Fasuko and her father to get away to a place of safety.

'Me an' my partner need to talk a little more,' said Casey. 'You git outside an' shift thet stiff into the barn. Don't try nothin'. We still got ya covered.'

Jerry stalked outside, neck an shoulders rigid. The prospect of handling the corpse of the young man filled him with dismay. If he had been asked to help lift the kid into a coffin he could have done that out of a sense of duty and respect but dragging the pitiful corpse into a derelict barn was something else. He bent down, trembling a little as he saw again the look of horror frozen into the young face.

When he came back into the house, both men were on their feet. Flynn was checking his rifle. Casey glared balefully at him as he closed the door.

'OK,' he rasped, 'we got a deal.'

'I was goin' to tell ya,' replied Jerry, 'part of the deal is thet the girl and her father are safe. If not, then there ain't no deal. They need to be left here in peace.'

Flynn shrugged looking over at Casey. 'Sure. The gal will be left in peace. What the hell.'

They spent some time loading up the fresh mule from the paddock with the stores that had just come in, an old army tent, blankets and cooking gear. Casey did much of the work while Fasuko carried out food from the kitchen. Jerry helped her until she noticed the blood dripping down his sleeve from the graze he had received from Casey's bullet earlier which had now opened up again. She took time to help him off with his shirt and to dress the wound with a clean bandage. Then she brought out an old shirt from a drawer and told him to put it on. It was a grey shirt of the kind worn by Confederate soldiers, faded now, but still carrying army buttons.

'It was in Coney's saddle-bag,' she explained. 'It is quite all right. I washed it.'

He nodded his acceptance, smiling a little as he looked into her eyes, which held an amused tenderness.

'I will never be able to thank you enough for what you have done,' she whispered. 'You must keep yourself safe also.'

He did not feel at all certain about that, but forced himself to whisper a confident answer, wondering at the same time to what extent she really understood the kind of men she had been sharing this house with. He felt that she must believe that he had a plan for his own survival and would shake off Casey and Flynn when the time came. or did she think that he really had learned something from his father about the gold but had not been quite straight with her?

Whatever her thoughts, she seemed to be accepting the situation calmly, although, of course she was greatly relieved at the prospect of at last making her way to safety and a new life with her father. He turned away with mixed feelings, thanking her for the bandage and the shirt, but with a growing sense of hurt that she could see him ride off with such happiness rising inside her heart. Seconds later he cursed himself for a fool. If he was not doing this for her happiness then why was he doing it? It all had to be for her, for her beauty, for her dignity and courage, for her self-sacrifice with regard to her father, and for the quiet tenderness which she was beginning to extend towards him.

The afternoon dragged on towards dusk. Casey and Flynn had decided to go under cover of the night because there was always the chance that somebody might be riding around, who would want to find out exactly who they were and where they were heading. There was a pretty good chance too that some of them or their kinfolk could by now be searching around for the kid. That thought nagged at their minds like a coyote digging into a prairie-dog hole and made them jittery and anxious to get going. But at the same time it made them too scared to try it while there was a flicker of light in the sky.

At last the red of the departing day vanished into the west, observed by Casey and Flynn from the yard, hands still at their gunbelts, eyes ever watchful. Overhead, stars were beginning to spangle the yawning vault of the night. A cold breeze sprang up, rustling the massed weeds of the long-neglected fields. Flynn nodded and pulled his jacket more closely around his vast bulk.

'Time to git goin'.'

'Yeah,' answered Casey. He waved the barrel of his Colt at Jerry. 'You git mounted up. Take your own horse.'

Jerry did so, wanting almost as much as they to get started, for the tensions of the long afternoon had dragged at his nerves.

'Now, you, Jappo.' The gun pointed steadily at the girl. 'You next. You're comin' too.'

'What the hell!' Jerry shouted out

loud, anger whipping through him. 'The deal was to leave her here!'

Flynn's gun was aimed straight at his heart.

'You got it wrong. We said she would be left in peace and so she will, when we git near the gold.'

'Then there's no deal! You kin forgit it! She's to stay here with her father.'

'Listen, numbskull.' Flynn was tense but at the same time, matter of fact, as if he was explaining the obvious. 'If we leave the gal here, then there's nothin' to stop her setting thet bunch from the ferry on our trail first chance she gits, an' thet's jest what she'll do, because she hates me an' my buddy jest as if we was a coupla' rattlesnakes. So, for that reason, we cain't leave her here. The other reason is thet she knows her way around this territory pretty good because she's lived here fer a long time, ever since she was a kid, an' kin set our noses fer Filey's Creek better then we kin. Me an' Casey ain't so sure, because there was a helluva lot of shootin' thet time an' we got lost in the woods and didn't know where we was until we sees the ferry an' remembered thet ol' Coney was headin' fer this place upstream aways. The gal kin lead us to Catamount Valley an' then we kin find our way easy to Filey's Creek. After thet, she kin git back here to see her ol' man. It's the only way any of this kin work out fer Casey an' me. If ya don't like it, ya kin take a bullet, an' she'll take one too, an' her ol' man. Casey an' me are movin' out an' we ain't wastin' any more time chewin' the fat about this or anythin' else. So what do ya say?'

Jerry said nothing. He looked over at Fasuko as she stood in the shadows of the building, and saw that she was standing straight and rigid, as if overcome with surprise and dismay. Then he thought he saw her nod slowly, as if resigned to the situation she could not help.

He knew there was nothing he could do either. Flynn and Casey were now desperate men. They meant what they said and he understood their reasoning.

The dead kid in the barn had tipped the game over and left him without enough chips to bargain with.

5

They made slow progress through the night, seeing their way only by the dim light of the stars, and retarded by the heavily laden mule. Fasuko went ahead of the little procession, staring straight to the front, seemingly deep in her own miserable thoughts, but still unerring in her judgement and sense of direction. Just behind her Casey rode, rifle across saddle, ready to punish with death any attempt to escape.

Third in line came Jerry, wrapped in a blanket of his own misery. He was guarded by Flynn, whose hand rested on the butt of a Colt .45, with a rope from his saddle-bow pulling along the reluctant mule in the rear.

Nothing was said. Only the plodding of hooves and the snorting of the animals broke the silence. Often, Jerry looked ahead to catch an occasional glimpse of Fasuko's black hat, pulled down now over her hair against the night cold. He knew that she was riding to her death as was he. These men had already demonstrated, in no uncertain terms, their ruthlessness and, in their way of thinking there was no reason why they should spare her once she had served her purpose. They might keep her alive until they arrived at Filey's Creek, knowing that it was the only sure way of ensuring his full cooperation. But once the gold was in their hands — or in truth, once they realized how they had been tricked — then the guns would blaze and they would die together. The thought filled him with dread. He knew he was just as afraid of dying as most men, but much worse was the image of her beautiful young form stretched out in ugly death, while these monsters grinned, spat and turned away.

He was so lost in thought he did not notice for the first hour or so the country over which they travelled was slowly rising and the faint outline of hills loomed to the south-east. The ground was becoming more rugged and Fasuko led them in little detours around steep rises and outcrops of rock. Here and there, trees, squat and twisted from the winds of the neighbouring prairies, stood in their way and forced them to brush aside grasping twigs and branches.

Towards midnight, Flynn grunted out a command to halt and then rode forward, his cautious eyes seldom leaving Jerry, and spoke to Fasuko.

'Don't know where the hell we are. What about the woods? Don't we go through the woods?'

'No.' Her voice floated gently through the night air with a calm that somehow brought a foolish sense of relief to Jerry. 'Maybe you went through woods before when you were lost but this is the way to Catamount Valley.' She pointed towards a little south of east. 'That way. Around the foot of these slopes.'

Flynn seemed satisfied and they went

on, while the stars swung slowly in a long circular voyage overhead. For the hundredth time, Jerry searched in his mind for some plan of escape that would have even the slightest chance of success but nothing came to him. Not now. Nothing was possible while nervous fingers hovered over trigger guards and nerves jumped at the faintest sound.

At last a hint of grey began to tinge the eastern sky with a promise of dawn. Flynn again called a halt, more confidently this time, as if he felt in less danger of discovery now. He dismounted, waving on the others to do the same, and then stretched his back, cursing with pain as he did so.

'Goddamn! I'm as sore as hell! Never thought a hoss could knock me around like this!'

'Too much sittin' on our backsides in thet stinkin' farm!' commented Casey. 'I'm jest the same. All this time outa' the saddle don't do an ol' cavalryman no good!'

'Thet's it,' agreed Flynn. 'Anyhow, time fer a break. Here, Jappo, git some coffee brewed up an' make it quick.'

'Think it's safe?' asked Casey. 'I mean, the fire?'

'Sure. We're well on our way. Anyhow, we kin hide the fire more or less in the rocks. Hey, jackrabbit!' He waved his pistol at Jerry. 'Git a fire started but keep it small an' well into the stones.'

Coffee was brewed while Flynn sat and grumbled and pummelled the muscles of his legs and lower back. Sometimes, he got to his feet and walked up and down, cursing and spitting as he went. Casey did not seem to be so badly affected and sat chewing at the bread which Fasuko had brought him from the packsaddle. He cut off slices with a bowie knife and stuffed them into his mouth as if he had not seen food in days.

'Hey, Jappo,' he mumbled through his full mouth, 'how far to go now afore we gits to Catamount?'

'About two hours. We go around that slope and over towards the top of that hill in the distance. The valley opens just on this side of it.'

'Gal knows her way around,' admitted Flynn. 'Maybe we could git a little bit o' shut-eye afore we move on. One at a time, o' course, an' not until I've had some breakfast. Hey, hand over some o' that bread, will ya? You gonna eat all of it?'

The bread was slung over with the knife and Flynn cut a thick slice and dropped the knife on a stone beside him. He rammed the bread into his mouth. 'Coffee! That coffee-pot not ready yet?'

Jerry was bending over the fire, balancing the pot over the flames. It was just about coming to the boil. His eyes were on Flynn and then they went to the knife and then to Fasuko, who stood a little to the rear. He saw she was looking at the knife too. Her face was expressionless, but there was an air of tension in her posture. He moved to a more upright position, glancing now away from her, and moved towards Flynn.

'Coffee's ready,' he said calmly. 'Pass over the mug.' Then he stumbled hard down upon one knee and the hot liquid shot out from the steaming can all the way over Flynn's leg.

'My God!' Flynn yelled in agony, mug flying, arms beating wildly in pain. 'Jeeze! Ya dumb bastard!'

His gun was in hand, pointing, and then he lashed out, striking Jerry hard across the shoulder with the barrel. Jerry fell to one side, pain shooting through his arm and collar bone. For a second he could not see through the mist of tears that obscured his vision, then he saw that both guns were trained upon him.

He knew he was suddenly as near to death as he had ever been, but he looked past Flynn to the stone where the knife had lain and saw that it had gone. He saw too, out of the corner of his eye, that Fasuko had stepped back quickly into the shadows near the horses.

'It was an accident!' He yelled as loudly as he could, willing Flynn and Casey to keep their attention upon him. 'How could I help it! Why don't ya git your own damned coffee? Ya lowdown coupla dead-beasts!' He shouted with all the strength he could muster, whipping up an assumed anger. 'If ya keep knocking me around I'm damned if I'll show ya where the gold is at all! You hear me? You'll never see the blasted gold!'

His mention of the gold just prevented them from pulling the triggers. They raged back at him, cursing him in the foulest terms imaginable, while he ranted as if on the point of madness. Then he saw Fasuko moving amongst the horses, like a shadow flitting from one to the other. Then she was up, mounted on her own horse, head and shoulders silhouetted briefly against the brightening sky, and the horse turned to gallop into the semi-dark.

'Goddamn!' Casey was on his feet, swinging with his Colt to let off a wild shot. He ran towards the horses, while Flynn rose clumsily to his feet to follow. Then Casey put a foot into the stirrup and slumped to the ground as the saddle slipped and fell. 'She's cut the cinch!'

It was the same with all three remaining horses — every cinch had been cut, swiftly, deftly, making rapid pursuit impossible.

For some minutes they stood in silence, wondering what to do, then Flynn swung his fist, hard and vicious, into Jerry's face, so that he almost stumbled into the fire.

'That was you! You an' yer damned coffee.' They were both staring at him again, murder in their eyes. He crouched rubbing his jaw, pain running through his body, the fear of death gathering around him, but still with his heart rejoicing at the thought of her escape.

Gradually, their anger subsided and

they set to repairing the cinches as best they could with lengths of cord and extra rope around the saddles. It wasn't much of a job. None of it could be mended in a satisfactory way without proper materials and fast riding was out of the question, but they reckoned that that hardly mattered since the laden mule was already such a drag on their progress.

They went on their way, Jerry to the front, feeling the threat of their guns on his back. The slope to the east rose up and then fell away and the pointed hill seemed nearer. The coolness of morning rapidly gave way to the heat of the day.

At length, the country opened out a little and green pasture rolled in front of them. To the east, smooth grassy slopes held groups of cattle, feeding quietly, undisturbed by their passage. In the middle distance, water caught the light of the sun.

'This Catamount?' Casey's voice was suddenly full of anxiety. 'Don't seem much like it to me. I heard tell thet Catamount was steep and rough! This cain't be it . . . '

His voice trailed off. Jerry followed his gaze up over the tumbling, pleasant landscape, with its background of low hills, and saw a white house gleaming like a beacon of invitation.

'Humblestream,' breathed Casey, his words scarcely audible. 'She was leadin' us here all the time.'

Jerry felt a tense rise of excitement. So she had been thinking of how to escape and had led them here, believing that the proximity of other people would give them both a chance, but the other opportunity had come and she had taken it.

'Come on, let's go.' Flynn was already turning back, pulling roughly at the mule's mouth as he did so. 'Best git the hell outa here, back the way we came. Lyin' bitch fooled us real good.'

Jerry was still looking up at the house. A figure had appeared in front of the white wall. A man, dressed mostly in black, put a hand to his brow and stared in their direction. He waved an arm and another figure, slightly shorter joined him. They both stood viewing for a few seconds and then they had gone.

Casey had seen them too. He put spurs to his horse as he turned and then grasped wildly at its mane as his saddle began to slip. With difficulty, he regained his seat but was forced to slow the animal down to no more than a walk.

'Damn the blasted Jappo she-wolf!' he yelled, exasperated out of his mind.

Jerry did not move, but then a gun was turned upon him and he knew he must follow or drop dead where he was.

The next time he glanced back he saw that a bunch of five horsemen were approaching at speed down the slope and must soon overtake them. His heart sang with delight in the knowledge that matters would soon be settled and Flynn and Casey would be handed over to the law. But he said nothing, knowing that he was not yet safe.

Within a very short time, his captors saw the futility of attempting to escape and came to a halt, determined to pretend innocence. At the same time, they warned Jerry that a wrong word from him would he his last.

The approaching horsemen slowed down as they drew near and spread out into a semicircle, rifles ready, eyes narrowed and faces stern. They were all dark-haired and three of them were heavily moustached. Four were young men but the leader was much older with greying hair. Jerry guessed at once that he was the father of at least two of them but it seemed a family resemblance ran through them all. Then he remembered Judy at the ferry and it all seemed to fall into place.

There followed a heavy silence, during which Flynn tried to appear nonchalant, and Casey gave a crooked smile that was supposed to be friendly. At length the older man spoke.

'Why are you Rebs trespassin' on my land?'

'Rebs? We ain't Rebs. We didn't know it was your land. Jest a mistake.' Casey spread out his arms as if in apology. 'We'll git goin' right away.'

'Ain't Rebs, eh?' One of the younger men grinned. He pointed straight at Jerry's shirt. 'I ain't never seen so many Reb uniforms since yeller-bellied Lee surrendered.'

For the first time it occurred to Jerry that he didn't look very different from the men he was with and if he opened his mouth he would sound like them too. His accent was just the same. To the Yanks, he might seem no different, just another Reb, like Flynn and Casey. He felt anger rise, not because he was seen as a Reb, but because he was being mistaken as a partner of such men.

'The war's over, ain't it?' Flynn was

doing his best to appeal to reason and hiding his nervousness as best he could.

'Maybe for some.' Another man had spoken, his speech slurred, and Jerry saw with a shock that the corner of his mouth had been extended in a long cut that had never healed. It carved into his features an ugliness which his moustache could not hide.

'You men from Broken Rock?' The older man was again speaking. 'You Smith and Brown?'

'Well, yeah, thet's right.' Casey saw the hopelessness of attempting to deny it, his mind on the dead youth in the barn, but praying that they could somehow talk their way out before the kid was discovered. 'We're jest movin' out now. Decided to git back home, south, ya know, after all this time. Gits kinda lonesome away from your own folks.'

'Thet so? You sure you're Smith and Brown? What about Coney and Casey and Flynn?'

The shock showed itself in Casey's face. Flynn twitched visibly. 'Don't know what ya mean,' he murmured, 'never heard of them.'

'Ya don't say!' The man with the scarred face glared, eyes somehow fanatical, burning like coals. 'Well, jest about everybody else has! You guys were at Filey's Creek, thet right?' He did not wait for a denial, the conviction in his voice refuting any argument. 'You stole the gold thet night an' got clear away with it too. I know. I was there! I was in the Union Army and was took prisoner thet same day. I heard my guards talkin' about it afore they sent me way behind the lines to the Reb prison camp. I heard them talkin' about all thet gold coin thet was meant to pay fer artillery and ammunition and stores fer the Confederates. I heard . . . '

His voice slurred off into incoherence and his head and shoulders trembled like those of a man whose nerves had been shot to pieces.

'It's OK, Jed.' The older man spoke

to him quietly as if to calm him down, and then turned to Flynn and Casey to continue the story. 'What my son's sayin' is thet a mule-train of the Southern army was near captured by the Union infantry. Most of it was shot up but the Reb cavalry who were meant to rescue it went off instead with a couple of mules carrying all the gold. Some of them deserters got killed by their own side but three escaped with all the stuff. The Reb Army searched around fer them for a while but then came the end of the war and everything was so mixed up thet nobody took up the trail of it — which was pretty cold anyhow. I guess nobody thought it was their responsibility any more. Jed heard about it in the Reb camps. It was in the papers too, at the end of the war but then it was forgotten about.'

'Yeah, an' then,' Jed had regained his composure and launched in again as if unable to keep out of it, 'then, jest a coupla days ago, my cousin, Judy, tells us thet some stranger at the ferry had been lookin' fer Coney. One of the deserters! We never thought thet the southern fellers up at Broken Rock was the same as them thet . . . '

'We ain't the same!' Flynn's protest carried no trace of conviction. 'We ain't no deserters!'

'Thet so?' The older man looked straight at Jerry. 'You look jest like the young feller my niece described. You one of the deserters lookin' fer your partner, Coney?'

'He was my cousin. I wanted to see him. I didn't know about any of this. I wasn't fighting near here at all!'

'Ya don't say. Well, well, and thet's the cleanest Reb shirt I've seen in a long time.'

'Hey, Cousin Henry!' A youth had ridden around to look more closely at the mule-pack. 'See what I found here — a spade! Could be they're goin' a'gold digging!'

The older man smiled. Something was creeping into his face and manner which went beyond that of an honest citizen inquiring into the truth. A light of greed had come into his eyes and suddenly Jerry knew that he and his family had no interest in bringing deserters and thieves to justice. All they were interested in was the gold.

'If we had known thet the gold was at Broken Rock we'd have paid you fellers a visit a long time ago.' Any pretence of honesty which might have existed was now rapidly dropped. 'If you have the gold in thet pack-saddle, then jest hand it over. If it ain't there, then you got about a coupla minutes to tell me where it is.' His grin broadened and he pointed his rifle into Flynn's chest. 'Think you better hand over your guns too.'

Flynn and Casey hesitated, but the circle of rifles was trained and steady, so they disarmed themselves with shaking hands.

6

'Let me explain somethin' to ya.' Henry had changed his rifle for a Colt .44 and now held it at Flynn's head. 'All of us were in the war. We all went in at the start, except fer Frank and my younger son, Billy, who was jest a kid — and still is — so we had it pretty rough and never got to likin' Rebs very much. I took a ball in the shoulder which jest about killed me and Jed here, got his face slashed by a bayonet from one of your Reb camp guards, jest fer the hell of it more or less, so we don't think we owe Rebs nothin', except maybe a good thrashing and if you're gonna be difficult about this here gold then I think Jed would jest as soon cut your head off even before I git through blowin' out your brains. So I reckon thet if you've any sense, you should start talkin', because gold ain't no good to a man after he's been decapitated.'

'I don't know where the stuff is!' Flynn's voice trembled. In his mind he kept wishing that he and Casey had not disarmed but had started shooting as soon as this bunch of crazy Yanks had appeared. That way, they might have had some chance, a slim one sure, but it might just have worked out. Now they had no chance of talking their way out of the situation because these men seemed to know too much and would obviously go to any lengths to get what they wanted. Even the law would have been better than this but when Bryce had asked this Henry character to bring in the sheriff he had just been laughed at.

'The gold was never at Broken Rock. Coney got rid of it before he went there.' Flynn's voice rose to a high-pitched whine. 'But he died. I told ya that! I never seen the stuff, but ask him! Ask thet Bryce gopher, sittin' there. He knows! He got a letter from

Coney. He knows where the gold is. His ol' man told him about it. Says it was hid somewhere's around Filey's Creek. Thet's where we was goin'. He was gonna show us where it's hid!'

'You were on your way to Filey's Creek!' Henry laughed sardonically, joined by his relatives. 'You sure have a side-winder's way of gittin' to Filey's Creek! What the hell are ya here fer if that's where you're goin'?'

'Blasted Jappo gal showed us wrong.'

'Jappo?'

'Chinee gal,' put in Frank. 'Maybe thet's it. She still up there at thet farm?'

'Yeah, least, I guess thet's where she's headed. Lit out on us this mornin' after we rode all night.'

'Ya rode all night from Broken Rock? How come it took ya so long? It ain't all thet far, is it? I thought maybe you set out this mornin'.' Henry seemed genuinely surprised. Realization came to Jerry. She had planned to get here in daylight when there would be a good chance of being seen. Had she known what this family was really like? Maybe they had just seemed a better bet than Flynn and Casey, and they wouldn't have had anything against her personally.

'This feller tellin' the truth? You know where the gold is?' Henry's dark eyes were boring into Jerry.

'No. I told them I knew but I don't.'

'Yeah? Who are you kidding? You ain't all jest riding out in the middle of the night with a pack-mule and spades and a tent and food fer nothin'. And don't tell me you all of a sudden got homesick!' Henry laughed dryly. 'So let's git down to business. See, this gold don't belong to you. It used to belong to the Confederate army but thet army was beat and doesn't exist any more. The Union army might have claimed it but they were never sure if it was fer real or if it was jest another story. I guess they've lost interest in it now because they ain't making no attempt to find it. Thet leaves you and us and you're jest thieves and deserters and ought by rights to be hung or shot. Me and my family, you might say, represent the Union army round here and so have a right to claim thet gold because we came out on the winning side and because we fought fer the north and lost a lot in the war and ain't never been compensated fer it.'

He smiled thinly as if he believed he could read Jerry's mind.

'So you reckoned you might jest git rid of these two fellers after you had led them the wrong way but you'll need to lead me straight to it because I ain't gonna be made a fool of. You still say it's at Filey's Creek?'

'It is,' replied Jerry. He could see that he was in exactly the same situation with the Galbraiths as he had been with Flynn and Casey, and the only thing to do was to go along with it in the hope that when the showdown came he might try to escape with his life. 'I do know where the stuff is.'

'Right,' decided Henry. 'Let's git goin'.'

They turned around and began to follow a narrow trail which drew them out of the fertile valley into more rugged country. They had not gone far when Louis Galbraith, a stockily-built man of about thirty at the head of the column called back to his uncle.

'Hey, Henry! Ain't seen young Billy this mornin'. He oughta be in on this! This kinda thing would send him crazy!'

'Sure. You're right. He wouldn't miss this fer anything,' answered his uncle. 'I thought maybe he had gone out ridin' early. Come to think of it, I ain't seen him since Jed and him went 'way downriver.'

'Well, he was with me at the ferry,' explained Jed. 'We stopped by on the way back a coupla nights ago, like I said. Had a chicken supper with Judy. Had to stay overnight. All of us talking about this here feller askin' about Coney. Billy was real wound-up about it, real excited. I came away early in the mornin' but he was keen to stay on and talk a bit more. Said he would follow after. Mean to say he ain't been around at all?'

'You ain't seen him, Mike?' Henry's voice held a hint of anxiety.

'Nope,' Mike shook his dark head, 'ain't seen him, Uncle Henry. Last I saw of him, he was on his way back to Humblestream. He went ahead of me. Thought he would have got home long before now.'

'Maybe still in bed. Not like him, though. He didn't seem ill or nothin'? Martha didn't say. Tell ya what, Frank, you jest turn around and git back to the house. Shouldn't take ya long and you kin easy catch up at the rate we're goin'. Tell him to come along with ya.'

Frank rode off at speed while the rest of the party continued at the slow pace dictated by the mule. The conversation had struck a chill into the hearts of Flynn and Casey and brought an overwhelming sense of trouble to Jerry. There was no doubt in any of their minds that young Billy Galbraith lay dead in the barn at Broken Rock and that the grim fact would very soon be dragged out into the open for all to see. It was likely to touch off an explosion in Henry Galbraith that would destroy the three of them. Jerry had asked for the sheriff to be brought in so that he could tell of the murder rather than this half-crazy story about the gold. Telling lies about the whereabouts of the Confederate gold seemed to him to be well justified in his initial effort to save Fasuko and his own skin, but to remain silent about that ghastly murder was something else. By doing so, he was lending support to the murderers and implicating himself. He would have to speak out. The consequences would be, in all probability, a quick bullet, but at least he would have told the truth and cleared his own conscience. He drew in his horse.

'Mr Galbraith. I'm sorry but I have

to tell you thet your son's dead. He came up to the farm yesterday. Fasuko, the Japanese gal there, recognised him, so I'm sure there's no mistake about it. These two men killed him because he seemed to know who they were.'

There was a stunned silence. Every horse was suddenly held in taut rein. The mule came to a stumbling stop and stood still. It seemed that no one could find breath, then Flynn yelled out, voice rising in panic.

'He's lyin'! It was him thet did it! He shot the kid! I tell ya it was him.'

All three were dragged from the loose saddles to the ground. Fists struck hard, boots thudded. The beating went on for a few minutes before Henry Galbraith could call a halt. Then Flynn and Casey and Jerry sat on the grass and stones. They were bruised, cut and gasping for breath. The Galbraiths stood around them, guns pointing at them, faces tense and shocked.

'The truth!' Henry almost screamed, his gun hand shaking. 'Tell me the truth about my son! You filthy rats!'

'It was him!' Casey waved a hand at Jerry, taking his cue from his partner. 'He killed the kid!' He bent over in a paroxysm of coughing, caused by a kick he had taken in the stomach. He rolled on the ground, spluttering and groaning. 'He did it! It was thet dirty skunk! We tried to stop him.'

He straightened up a little, holding his stomach. Something had fallen from his pockets: a pipe, an old piece of silver watch-chain and another object, a small silver star on a slip of leather.

'Thet's Billy's star.' Mike bent to pick it up. 'He always carried it on his hoss harness. Belonged to his grandpa.'

'You damned fool!' Flynn shook a fist at Casey. 'What the hell did ya have to take thet fer?'

Henry Galbraith's finger whitened on the trigger, then he hesitated.

'Shootin's too good fer you people.' His voice could hardly be heard but hissed like some deep underground fissure from hell. 'I'm goin' to ride out to git my son and on the way back here, I'm goin' to think about what to do with you animals. You kin expect slow burning, nothin' better than thet.'

'It wasn't us!' Flynn yelled louder than ever and lurched to his feet, making an unnecessarily aggressive movement. 'It was this Bryce bastard.'

He screeched as Mike pulled the trigger and sent a bullet into his side. He fell groaning, his blood oozing from the wound.

'Leave it, Mike!' shouted Henry. 'I said thet shooting's too good fer them. I'll decide when I've looked into Billy's face jest how long they should take to die. And anybody else who was there at thet farm. The Chinee gal too. You stay here, Jed, and keep them covered. Frank will be back pretty soon. If they give any trouble, fill their legs full of lead so they cain't move.'

Within a moment he had led Mike and Louis out of sight, cutting around a rugged, boulder-strewn slope. Flynn lay moaning upon the ground. Casey sat staring blindly, lips moving, lost in a bitter world of his own. Jed sat upon a boulder, gun at the ready, eyes studying Jerry, whose face blanked suddenly in renewed shock.

It was Henry Galbraith's mention of the Chinee gal that had struck hard into his soul. What if Fasuko were still at the farm? She had barely had time to get back there and help her aged father to get things together so as to get away. The Galbraiths might get there before she could escape. When they saw the dead kid there would be no stopping their desire for revenge and she would be the first to suffer the consequences. He groaned inwardly and looked up to see Jed's dark, cold eyes upon him.

The madness which had hovered and darted behind those eyes seemed to have settled. Now they held reason and calculation. A couple of times he licked his lips as if about to say something but changed his mind. It was as if there was some kind of a risk lying in front of him which he was unsure about challenging. Jerry looked back steadily, his right hand groping under his shirt.

'You,' Jed spoke softly almost as if afraid of being overheard. 'I reckon you know about this gold better than anybody, thet right?'

Jerry nodded, fingers stretching and crawling.

'Better than these two fellers, who don't know much, if anythin', or they wouldn't have been all this time makin' up their minds about looking fer it — thet right?'

'Yeah, I guess so,' replied Jerry steadily, nails prodding.

'Thing is, my pa rode outa here jest now with the feeling thet Billy might be still alive. He still has a bit of hope. I could see it in him. He doesn't want to believe it, but when he is sure Billy's dead then he'll do what he says. You'll all die — slowly. The Chinee gal too and her ol' man. That's all you've got ahead of you. He'll kill you sure — gold or no gold.'

'I'll lead ya to the gold,' put in Casey, seeming to awaken suddenly and anticipating what was to come.

'Shut your mouth,' snarled Jed, the madness flashing again, gun threatening. 'You, Bryce, if ya lead me to it, I'll give ya a share and let ya go. I heard there's a helluva lot of it, enough to make a lot of men rich, thet right?'

'Yeah,' answered Jerry, nails tearing, face set.

'Well, why shouldn't I have it?' Jed asked the question of himself as if seeking to square his conscience. His cut mouth drooped, yawning and ugly. 'I been knocked around enough, I guess. Listen, I know a place up in the hills we two kin hide out until pa and the rest of them quit searchin' round. No good goin' straight fer it right now because Filey's Creek is the first place they'll look when they see us gone. But we need to hurry before Frank gits back here.'

'What about me?' snarled Casey.

99

'What do ya say, Bryce? It's the only chance you'll get.' Jed's voice held anxiety and rising irritation.

'Right, I agree,' groaned Jerry, twisting on to his side. His finger nails were under the bandage, ripping out the scab which had formed over the bullet graze. Blood poured from it, over and through the pulled bandage and soaked his sleeve. He rolled further, pressing his body into the mess. Then he turned to show the blood over his shirt front. Jed pushed himself up and stepped forward, surprise in his face.

'Hey, are you hurt? You wasn't hit by Mike's . . . '

He bent over, peering, gun hand drooping a little. Jerry pushed upwards from a crouching position, legs propelling his body, head and neck ready for the shock. His forehead butted into Jed's jaw, slamming it shut, jerking back his neck. Concussion caused Jed's brain to black out for a few vital seconds. He reeled and fell, gun flying. Jerry leapt for it but Casey got there first. He snatched up the Colt and turned it on Jerry, mouth twisted into a snarl.

'So, ya thought you would put it over on me, did ya? Here it comes polecat!' He aimed at Jerry's chest, delight leaping into his face. But then his expression changed as did his aim as he looked past Jerry's shoulder. Instinctively, Jerry turned a little too and caught sight of Frank Galbraith drawing his mount to a hurried stop at the nearest bend of the trail. The young man went for his gun but he was too late. Casey fired quickly, grazing the horse's neck with one bullet and caving in Frank's chest with the next.

At that moment Jerry leaped into the attack, grabbing for Casey's gun hand. But Casey held on and they fell to the ground, clawing and punching. The wounded horse was bucking and trampling around, maddened with pain. A hoof struck into Jerry's shin, another hit Casey on the shoulder. Jerry rolled over, trying to protect his face, twisting his hand with the gun under his body.

Jerry felt his grip fail and he pulled himself free and hauled himself to his feet. With another wild whinny of fear, the horse made off, back the way it had come. Jerry ran then, desperation driving the pain from his body, until he reached his own horse and he dragged himself up into the slipping saddle and turned its head to follow the trail of Henry Galbraith.

A bullet sang past his head. Casey was kneeling ready to put in a more careful shot. Jerry took a fearful glance back and saw Jed get up and shamble towards the figure. Another shot rang out, panicky and wild. Then they came to grips, wrestling to the death.

Jerry did not stay to see more. He rode on, his mind full of thoughts of Fasuko's danger, the desperate fight falling away behind him. Ahead, the ground opened out a little into waving grassland that rolled gently downwards to the west. The tracks left by the Galbraith's three horses were easy enough to follow, the bent blades rising slowly towards the warmth of the sun. He rode as quickly as he could, balancing himself in the unsteady saddle, but finally it slipped, the stirrup swinging below the horse's belly so that he tumbled to the ground. He held grimly to the reins fearful that the animal would bolt and Fasuko would be left in danger.

He held the horse firmly, calming its fears better than he could his own, and then stripped the saddle and its useless ropes and cords from its back and threw them aside. He remounted, gently and gingerly, and lay tight along the horse's neck, gripping the reins and the mane, and went on his way bareback.

He could make no greater progress than a carefully controlled trot, slowing down often to a walk as he sought to calm the beast's nerves. The sun swung high towards noon and he had no idea how far there was yet to travel.

His mind was possessed by thoughts of Fasuko. He must get to Broken

Rock in time to save her. What he could actually do when he got there, he had no idea, but he must try to help her at whatever cost.

He had no gun, his body ached from its bruises and cuts, his arm bled unheeded, fatigue rose like a flood in his mind to drown him, and hope was slipping from him with every step of his tiring horse.

7

Sometime in the afternoon, when he was riding slowly up a long slope, he heard the sound of a rifle shot booming out from up ahead. He drew in his horse and listened intently. It came again, threatening and nerve-chilling but with its distance and direction disguised by the undulating ground. He went on at a creeping pace, urging his nervous and jittery mount to make its way up the rise but without losing control even for a second, for that lost second, he knew, might be his last if he blundered out into view of those hot rifles.

He topped the rise a little unexpectedly just the same and instinctively ducked his head as he saw the roof of the farmhouse standing out against the broad sweep of the river. He dropped to the ground and left his horse where it was, having no way of making it secure, and crawled forward through the grass until the house came more directly into view. At first, he could make out nothing unusual but then he saw that two windows on the side facing him were broken and a goat lay dead in the yard. The mule which Fasuko had brought back from her last trip to McCarry stood towards the rear of the building, harnessed and ready to go, but unmoving as if still tethered. For the moment, all was still. The riflemen, he reckoned, were peering down from their positions, ready to pick out the target when it moved.

That target, he knew for certain, was Fasuko. There was no one else who could attempt to resist them. The knowledge filled him with dismay and the idea that she might already be dead trod into his mind with crushing force. He was relieved a split second later when another rifle shot cracked from the house and a puff of smoke lingered for a moment at the window.

Cautiously, he strained his head and neck so as to look over to his left and a little downhill towards the spot at which Fasuko had appeared to aim. There was nothing to be seen but a sea of green weeds and a stretch of fencing.

He ducked again and crawled like a snake through the long grass. Gradually the grass gave way to tangled weed and he struggled on through, doing his utmost to make no sound. When he felt he had gone a fair distance, he raised his head and saw a horse, fully saddled, standing motionless up to the stirrups in greenery. With a sudden jolt of surprise and hope he saw that it still carried a rifle in the saddle-boot.

For a moment he did not dare breathe, but then he turned towards it, stalking and crouching like some predator seeking to make a kill. For all his caution the animal caught sight of him through the corner of an eye and jerked nervously away. He tried again, more slowly and without sound, but his every movement sent it further from him until at last it trotted off well out of reach, snorting and shaking its head.

He cursed under his breath and turned again in the general direction of the house and almost at once came across a trail through the weeds as if some person had gone before. He followed it, his every sense on the alert, expecting at any moment to find himself in hand-to-hand combat with one of Fasuko's attackers. Soon, he was crawling along by the wire fence. A few minutes later his hand touched a boot in the twisted jungle of undergrowth.

For one second, he hesitated and then jumped into his attack, only to come to a stumbling halt over the prone form lying face upwards, neck propped against the wire.

It was Mike Galbraith, jacket soaked in blood, eyes clouded and dying. At the sound of Jerry's shocked breath, those eyes opened a little further. Then the lips moved.

'Chinee gal . . . opened up on us right off . . . soon as we rode up.' There came a cough, then the eyes cleared a little and showed a faint gleam of recognition. The hand formed a weak fist and swung on an arm like a straw in the wind.

'Stinking Reb! Goddamn southern . . . '

The words died in his throat. Jerry lifted the pistol that lay in the grass and went on his cautious way along the fence, keeping his head still well down, eyes and ears keen, some cold, leaden weight inside pressing his nerves into compliance. A rifle boomed again from somewhere over towards the paddock. He pushed on faster, believing things must soon come to a head for it seemed obvious to him that the girl could not hold off two determined men for much longer. A gap appeared in the fence and he swung through it, putting a hand on one of the posts to steady himself. It gave way, its rotten foot cracking under his weight. His boot slipped on the slope and in a sudden unthinking movement he straightened himself up, holding on to the post as he did so.

A rifle bullet sang past his ear and smashed a large piece of rotten timber into smithereens. The report followed and he saw the smoke cloud appear again at the farmhouse window. Then he saw a man ahead of him, just a few yards further downhill, and Louis Galbraith turned towards him, alarmed by the smashing wood and twanging wire, rifle swinging to its new target.

Jerry lifted Mike's pistol. He pulled the trigger, once, twice, in rapid succession, but there was nothing — just the spinning chamber of an empty weapon. Louis stared amazed, realization dawning on his face for what seemed slow, slow seconds, then he tilted the rifle just a fraction, pointing it up the slope to pin-point the centre of Jerry's body.

In that moment, Jerry felt himself hanging on to his own life as if he was holding on to a precipice from which his fingers were slipping. Louis smiled grimly and raised himself up, steadying himself for the recoil of the rifle held at hip level. The smile stayed on his lips as the back of his skull caved in under the thunder of the heavy bullet and his blood-filled hat blew forward, scattering its contents.

Jerry crouched transfixed, and then scrambled over the trembling corpse to pick up the rifle. His hands were smeared in blood as he gripped the weapon and slid further down the incline to the shelter of a low bush.

Peering through the twigs and leaves, he had a good view of the house which seemed suddenly much closer. The windows had little glass left in them, the walls were pitted with fresh bullet holes. The battle had been going on for some time and Fasuko had been giving a good account of her courage and determination. The bullet that had killed Louis and the one that had come so close to him a moment before had came from her rifle. Obviously she had not recognized him as he had briefly appeared at the fence and her nerves must have been attuned to shoot at anything that moved, convinced, as she must have been, that she was surrounded by enemies. He felt that, if he could join her in the house, he could give her the support she needed and between them they could beat off the attack. After all, there was only Henry Galbraith left alive to oppose them. He was no mean opponent, but it was still just one against two. If he, Jerry, stood up and waved his arms, surely she must recognize him now. He did not look anything like a Galbraith. He was about to try this but changed his mind at the thought that he might also be seen by the enemy, so instead, he slipped through the bush and began another cautious descent, resolving to straighten up and run the last few yards across the open space near the house.

He had not far to go and was thinking of breaking into a sprint for the nearest window when a rifle cracked again just beyond the paddock. He saw the puff of smoke rising from an outcrop of broken rock which was just visible over the top of two low-lying wooden outbuildings.

Jerry stopped dead to size up the situation. The fact that Henry Galbraith was still firing at the house from that angle seemed to suggest he was not unaware of the presence of Jerry or of the death of Louis. Certainly, he must have heard the shots from that side of the house but would probably have believed that his cousin was still keeping up his fire to hold Fasuko's attention while he moved in from the paddock end. Now, no doubt, he had caught sight of the girl near the back door and had put in another shot in the hope of bringing the duel to a close.

To run into the house would provide immediate support for Fasuko, if he could do so without being hit, but it now seemed he could work his way around behind Galbraith, quite unseen, and finish him off. It was a decision that required little consideration, and Jerry turned again and scrambled up the grassy slope and through the fence into the field of weeds. There, he worked his way well back until he could no longer see the roof of the farmhouse and went into a low, crouching run through the tangled growth to gain a position parallel to the rocky outcrop. Jerry realized crawling along slowly, as he had done before, would be dangerous this time. Pretty soon, he guessed, Galbraith would be moving in for the kill or would strike lucky with a long shot and that would be the end of Fasuko and of everything.

He was out of breath by the time he judged it right to change direction, but slowed down only slightly as he came in sight once again of the river and the homestead. The wooden sheds were now fairly close and blocked his view of the paddock and the rocks he had believed Henry Galbraith to be lying behind. Within minutes he had made his way to the back of the nearest shed and slipped cautiously past, glancing through the door as he did so. Like a lot of places around the farm, it smelled damp and musty. An assortment of harnesses hung on hooks on the wall. A moment later, he was at the corner of the rough building and peered round the edge.

Galbraith had moved forward some way from the rocky outcrop and was now crouching behind a large boulder near the paddock. Beyond him, the mule still stood placidly, harnessed to something that Jerry could not see clearly and had no interest in at that moment. Henry Galbraith was prepared to take another shot. His rifle barrel slid a little to one side of the boulder. His eye was concentrated on the gun-sight. For a long moment, he did not stir a muscle and Jerry knew he was expelling his breath to make his aim the steadier. Jerry felt he had little time for such finesse. He raised the rifle with its bloody trigger guard and took swift aim. A split second later he pulled the trigger. Galbraith fired at the same moment and the double crash of sound reverberated around the rocks and buildings. To his chagrin, Jerry realized he had missed. His bullet spun across the paddock, twanging a wire on the other side.

At that moment a piercing scream came from the farmhouse. Galbraith's shot had smashed its way through a panel of the door and Jerry knew at once that Fasuko had been immediately behind it and had suffered a terrible wound. The shriek came again, a little lower in tone now, but carrying an intensity of agony. His heart seemed to burn and crumble. The pain that shuddered through him could hardly have been greater had he felt the impact of the bullet himself. For a moment he was stunned and unable to react. Then hatred rushed into his mind and he raised the rifle again, training it upon Galbraith's back as he rose from his hiding-place.

All Henry Galbraith's attention was on the door. Jerry's shot, drowned out by his own, had gone unnoticed. He advanced with long strides and with little caution, sure now that the combat with this fierce girl had come to an end. Jerry pulled the trigger but there was no cartridge. He swung the weapon round to hold it as a club and then run up behind Galbraith, overtaking him in seconds.

However, Galbraith heard the sounds of his approach, and turned to meet him. The dark eyes opened wide in astonishment and then flashed with anger. The rifle whirled ready to fire but Jerry was too close for aim to be taken and both weapons jarred heavily. Jerry swung again, this time catching his opponent's hand so that his knuckles split and bled. Galbraith snarled in pain and fury and struck out, hammering into Jerry's elbow, while another bullet sang into the sky.

Jerry knew that he must not continue with this kind of fight. A little space, the slightest opportunity, and Galbraith's next bullet would find its mark. His left arm was numbed from the blow on the elbow and his right hand could not use the heavy rifle as a club to any effect. He dropped it and threw himself at Henry Galbraith, head down, butting, arms swinging to get some kind of a grip around the body.

His head thumped into his opponent's stomach, almost driving the breath out of him. Henry Galbraith though was a big man, tall and heavy, and not easily felled. He staggered but did not go down at once. Desperately, Jerry drove into him, pushing hard with his feet into the stony ground, seeking to overbalance his enemy, to knock him to the earth and to make him drop his gun.

They swung around in a half-circle, Jerry almost losing his footing, his boots scraping the soil and pebbles. In a second, he knew he would be getting the worst of it. Henry Galbraith, using his superior weight and strength, must throw him off, strike him aside with the rifle. Then would come the final shot that would put paid to him and end any hope for Fasuko.

And, in his heart, he still held some hope for Fasuko. In spite of the scream and that piteous wail, he still hoped, against all the odds, that she had not been fatally wounded and if he could survive this brutal conflict, he could do something for her. It was that thought that drove him on and forced him not to let go while there was still a chance of coming out alive.

He threw himself forward once again, head butting as low as he could. At the same time his leg curled around that of Galbraith, leather boot to boot, and he pushed with all his weight, his own feet lifting off the ground as he felt his opponent topple, tripping backwards out of control, falling like a tree under the axe.

Galbraith hit the ground with a tremendous thump, much of the force in his lower back although Jerry's hands took some of the impact. He expected to stop there, to struggle free for that vital second and to get his hand upon a stone and with luck, strike before Henry Galbraith could recover. But it did not happen like that. The fall did not stop. It went on, down and down, both overbalancing, even from that prone position, heads first into some dark depths.

They slid, Galbraith backwards, and Jerry forwards, into a pit until only their legs remained above the surface. They came to a sudden jarring, cracking halt. All was dark. Jerry had a fearsome sensation of being buried alive. He was jammed between the side of the pit and the body of Galbraith, the breath knocked out of him, unable at first to move.

For a long moment, he lay quite still, his brain refusing to function. Then his senses cleared a little and he wrenched his arms free from around Galbraith's waist and pushed with all his might. There was nothing to push against except the chest of his adversary as the sides of the pit gave way at every touch. Slowly, he eased himself a few inches, backing upwards, scraping with the toes of his boots for a hold on the level earth above. Every movement brought a spasm of pain in his jarred elbow but he hardly noticed it in his desperation to climb back out of the darkness. Showers of earth and small pebbles rattled over his head. His hand gripped Galbraith's gunbelt and he thrust against it and gained a couple of feet. Then he was clear, sliding backwards across the surface and struggling to his knees.

Henry Galbraith lay still at the bottom of the deep hole, his face turned upwards, his neck broken. His mouth gaped a little and his eyes were half-open. Earth had fallen into his moustache and mouth, but he did not stir.

Jerry did not rise to his feet at once. He was out of breath and his nerves felt shattered. For a little while he could not move. Then he shook some of the dirt from his hair and eyes and looked around. The deep hole was in front of him. The spare mule stood a few yards away. It was still attached by a thick rope to the massive corner post that had served the paddock but which had now been taken out. Stones of various sizes, some of considerable weight, were scattered all around. The wire cut from the post was twisted and tangled in confusion.

He stared at the mess uncomprehendingly and then felt a surge of joy at the realization that the battle with the Galbraiths was over, but the sensation was short-lived as the memory of Fasuko's scream came flooding back into his mind. In a moment he was on his feet and hurrying towards the door. It was, of course, locked, and he knocked hard upon it with his fist and called out her name to no effect.

He stood for a moment longer, nonplussed, head still spinning, and then hurried towards the river side of the building as he remembered there was another door there. When he reached the corner he stopped again, breathing hard to clear his head, and looked towards the river. The short, wooden jetty was partly covered by a scattering of bags and bundles, obviously dropped in haste. At the far end was the broad boat, still tightly moored but straining in the current. To Jerry's astonishment, the old man sat upright near the stern, wearing a wide hat and heavy coat, staring calmly across the water as if deep in thought and seemingly unaware that anything had been happening.

Jerry's first impulse was to call out but he immediately changed his mind. The old man seemed to be at peace for the moment. Soon would come the rude awakening when he had to be told of his beloved daughter's death or he would be called from his reverie to watch her die from her wound.

The door on this side of the house was slightly ajar. It was apparent that Fasuko had been carrying their belongings from the house to the boat just before the arrival of the Galbraiths had forced her to reach for her rifle and defend herself and her father.

God, what a fight she had made! His admiration was laced with amazement that a girl, so small, light, tender and quiet of voice, could have fought with such courage and skill. In the end, though, it had all gone against her and she had suffered the terrible wound that made her cry out in agony and despair. He cursed himself for having arrived too late to make any material difference in the fight except perhaps to nurse her now in her dying moments and to help her aged parent in any way he could. God, how he cursed Casey and Flynn and all of them for their greed for gold and their cruelty.

He advanced towards the door and pushed it open, hesitating before entering, afraid of what he was about to see. Then he braced himself and went in. A figure moved towards him through the interior. He halted, gasped, and then breathed a great sigh of relief. Fasuko walked to the door, a bundle under her arm, rifle still in hand.

She smiled with no trace of hurt, fear or surprise.

'You are all right?' Her voice was calm, almost unconcerned. 'I was hoping that you had not been hurt.'

He could not answer at once. Amazement and incredulity competed with unbounded joy making him tongue-tied. When he spoke at last, he found himself stammering in a way that he never had done before.

'I-I thought — it seemed like-like — you were hit! He fired through the — door. You screamed like you were dying! I thought ya must be ba-badly wounded. Dead maybe . . . '

She looked at him steadily and then shrugged, her dainty shoulders emphasizing the grace of her every movement.

'I tried to draw him out,' she said, 'so that I could kill him but you messed it up.'

She waited politely until he remembered his manners enough to step aside to let her past, and then she walked to the end of the jetty and placed the bundle and the gun on board the boat. Some remark was made to her father in his own language which made him look round and smile and then she turned and began picking up the rest.

'Perhaps you could help me to get these things on to the boat?'

He nodded and began to walk down the jetty. Something was starting to fall into place. He stopped half-way along and looked back around the side of the house towards the paddock. The mule was still standing patiently, flicking its ears at the flies, and firmly anchored to the corner post. Henry Galbraith's legs showed out over the top of the old post-hole. Beyond that, the rocky escarpment stretched to the sky.

'Jerry! Can we hurry?' Her voice had become a little more insistent, then it hinted at apprehension. 'What are you looking for? There are no more of them are there? No more men coming?'

'No, no, there ain't no more.' He

smiled at her for the first time, oddly pleased that she seemed to be appealing to him. He bent down to lift a bundle of clothing and when he straightened up he saw her staring intently towards the rocks.

He followed her gaze. Jed Galbraith was riding at speed through the jagged escarpment, pistol in hand and his face a mask of rage.

8

Jerry stood stock-still for a moment, surprise and consternation spreading across his features. Somehow, to see Jed Galbraith now was like seeing a man who had risen from the dead. He had felt that the fight with Casey had had an air of finality about it and that neither could survive. They had seemed desperate, hate-filled opponents, bent upon killing one another. He saw now that this idea had been prompted by his own wish, for he had known that he had many fierce enemies ahead of him and could stand no more at his back.

Casey, though, had obviously got the worst of it and Jed had now come to help his father and seek revenge. He was coming down the slope, weaving his way through the rocks, his eyes on Jerry, pistol up and ready to fire.

The movement of the threatening

gun jerked Jerry into action. There was not a second to lose. He turned to look at Fasuko.

'Let's have the rifle, quick!'

She was already on board the boat and was in the act of untying the rope which came away with no more than a sharp pull.

'The gun, Fasuko, quick!'

'No, no.' She glanced at him then at Jed Galbraith. 'We must go.'

A bullet from Jed's pistol hit the jetty leaving a streak of torn surface-wood. Jerry stared at her, wondering what she meant then he realized that the Colt .45 at that range was likely to be inaccurate. A lucky shot might hit one of them but probably not. In a very few moments, though, all that would change. A gun battle at the end of the jetty against the water would have them at a severe disadvantage and Fasuko had her father to think of as well as herself. If Fasuko could get well away from the bank she could use the rifle to advantage, because of its longer range and better accuracy, and Jed Galbraith would also have a moving target to contend with. He began to run along the boards towards the boat. Suddenly, she looked at him, dismay written across her face.

'Jerry! Jerry! The bag! Throw me the bag!'

He stopped short, almost stumbling, and looked wildly round. There were various bundles and household utensils scattered at his feet. An oriental-looking umbrella was stuck between the planks while an old fishing-rod hung over the water. None of it looked of much value but there was a bag lying just a little way from which he had already stepped over on his way towards the boat. He bent down to it swiftly and realized by its queer, bumpy shape that it was full of ornaments from the house and when he knocked it with his boot, it sounded metallic. At the top. partly concealed, was the little brass Buddha which he had seen the old man polishing. Of course, the old fellow would want this, but was it worth the increased risk of a bullet?

He grabbed the bag and staggered to the end of the jetty. The boat had moved out a little further and he had to swing the bag with an effort to get it aboard and then he jumped, striking his shins on the gunwale and toppling into the boat. Another shot rang out, nearer this time. Fasuko had her head down and was pushing off hard from the jetty, using the long sculling oar. The boat swept out to catch the current. Fasuko slipped the oar back into its notch by the stern-post and threw herself into a graceful and rhythmic side-to-side movement which pushed them well out into the water.

Even so, they were not yet out of range, even of the Colt, and Jerry glanced back anxiously. Jed Galbraith had, he saw with some surprise, brought his horse to a stop some distance from the jetty. He was up near the paddock and was no longer concentrating upon them but was staring down into the posthole. He did not move. It was as if all his body and mind had frozen. The horror of the situation struck Jerry, turning his thumping heart cold. For the first time, it came to him, the corpse stuck down there, in all its ugly twistedness, was not just a man but also a man's father.

The thought weighed down his mind so that for some minutes he could not think beyond it. Only when Jed jerked his horse around and urged it towards the jetty did Jerry become alert to a new danger, for Jed had with him a rifle which he drew from the saddle-boot.

He reached over and pulled Fasuko's rifle up from the bottom of the boat. He saw, with no great surprise, it was an old cavalry gun of the kind his father had brought back from the war. It had, he reckoned, belonged to Cousin Coney. And it was loaded too. He knew that without checking for she had not been kidding when she had said she had been on the point of killing Henry Galbraith. He put it to his shoulder and turned it towards Jed.

He saw at once Jed was having difficulty. His horse was standing steady. The rifle was in his right hand but he could not raise it to his shoulder. His left arm hung down limply although he was obviously trying with all his might to lift it to the barrel of the gun. He tried over and over again but with no success, then he dropped the rifle to the ground. He crouched over his horse's neck, head hanging, shoulders shaking in pain and distress.

Jerry did not fire. He could not.

The boat was almost in the centre of the river, following the current and urged on by Fasuko's sculling. Her face was set in thought. She did not look at him or back at their mutual enemy. Her father sat staring benignly at the water. Jerry looked from one to the other. He was relieved at their escape. When he thought of what might have happened, he felt overjoyed to see them in safety but he was puzzled by the lack of response to their sudden good fortune. He could just about understand the old man, who seemed to have little idea what was going on, but from Fasuko he would have expected something different. Still, he thought, she was doing what made good sense. She was moving the boat downriver as fast as she could. It was like her — calm and practical.

When he looked back along the river-bank, he saw that the little farmstead was dropping away behind them, already beginning to look less real. He saw the dead goat in the yard and two horses in the fields, one of them his own. Then he saw Jed Galbraith coming around the side of the house and urging his horse into a gallop along the bank. Jerry did not know much about boats but he did know about horses and it was obvious to him that the animal could not keep up that pace for very long. Nevertheless, the boat was not travelling very fast and it seemed quite likely that Jed might push his mount to its limits so that it could draw level with the boat. Then the shooting must start again.

He watched with the utmost concentration and within a few minutes realized his guess had been right. They had not seen the last of Jed. The first shot rang out when the horseman had approached to within easy pistol range but it went wide just the same and the one after was no more accurate. Even at that distance Jerry could see that Jed's arm was shaking whenever he lifted the gun. Also his horse was faltering, snorting and slowing down. With the rifle, Jerry could have shot him down easily but he could see no sense in adding to the carnage.

'Bryce!' Jed's voice was weak but carried across the silent water. 'You murdered my father! You murdered my father! You murdered him!'

It was not true. It was nowhere near true but the anguish in the man's voice made it sound as if it might be. There were tears running down his haggard features. He slumped across the horse's neck and his pistol fell from his grasp. He swayed, grabbed wildly at the pommel and then toppled to the ground while his horse shook its mane and turned away to the sweet-smelling grass.

Jerry looked into the bottom of the boat where water swirled around the soles of his boots. For many minutes there were no clear thoughts in his mind and no words came to his lips. When at last he looked up he found Fasuko was watching him closely and he had the impression that she had been doing so for a while. She smiled, lifting his spirits, and he smiled at her in return.

'The world is full of sorrow, Jerry,' she said.

He nodded his agreement and then shrugged his shoulders, trying to shake off a sense of depression. She was no longer sculling but using the oar only to steer, keeping the boat straight. Around her feet were all sorts of oddments gathered in her flight from the house. On the thwart near her there were two bulging canvas bags, old and partly rotted, damp-looking too. One of them showed a glint of yellow metal through a small hole in its side. He had noticed them when he first came aboard but had been too taken up with events to look at them carefully. Now he did so without surprise because he knew what they were and had done so ever since he had watched Jed Galbraith looking down into that post-hole.

'Thet the gold ya got there, Fasuko?'

She was silent for only a brief moment before answering. 'Yes, Jerry, it is.'

'It was under the corner post thet ya dug up?'

'Yes. You see, when the war started the people who lived at Broken Rock were replacing some of the paddock fence. When they came to dig out for the gate-post they hit stone and had to dig deep and wide. They did not finish

137

it before they went away. They left the hole and the new post. When Coney came he forced me and my father to help him bury the gold under the post and then fill in the hole with stones and cover it over with earth. I think he meant to kill us afterwards but then he became too weak from his wound and died just after the arrival of Flynn and Casey. So it was there all the time.'

'And ya never really wanted to leave Broken Rock, did ya, over all thet time?'

'No, why should it be left for someone else to find? It does not belong to anyone except us.'

Jerry felt he had heard some kind of argument like this before.

'So you were always jest waiting for a chance.'

'Yes, all I needed was some time — a little time to dig it out.'

He could imagine, he could see in his mind's eye, the labour she had carried out to get to it. She had shifted all of those heavy, awkward stones herself, dragging them out at an almost impossible angle. Even with the help of the mule to haul the post, it must have been an exhausting task, especially with the need to make haste in case anybody else should come to rob her of it.

'That was what the letter was all about, Fasuko, to make some time?'

She laughed suddenly, her gaiety infectious enough to make him join in.

'Yes, you see I found a letter from your father in Coney's pocket — in his spare shirt. I thought that if your father came to Broken Rock, or even sent a letter back to his cousin and mentioned the gold being at Filey's Creek, even if he denied knowing anything about it, it would be enough to start them thinking that it might be somewhere else and nowhere around the farm at all. They might even have gone to Bluewater to ask your father about it. I am so sorry Jerry, but I did not know your father had died too.'

'Yeah, yeah, but if ya had got no answer, what then?'

'I would have tried again. I would have tried some other way. I would have found a way — in time.'

She would have done too, he knew that about her. It also occurred to him that if his father had been alive and had gone to Broken Rock, he might have placed himself in danger just as he had but then the girl had been desperate.

'Casey and Flynn threatened ya at first, didn't they? Maybe at other times too?'

'Yes, at first, but then they thought I knew nothing.'

'They made ya swear on the Bible. Thet's what ya said.'

'Yes, but what is the Bible?' she shrugged.

He nodded his understanding, remembering the little yellow Buddha, and looked at the banks of the river as they drifted slowly by. The farmstead had fallen out of sight but he found himself wondering again about Jed

Galbraith. He had looked like a dying man as he fell from that horse. It wasn't always easy to know what was right and what was wrong. That was something that he was beginning to realize more strongly than he had before. Things didn't always fit as neatly as bits of fencing into notch-holes. More often they had to be hammered and twisted to make them fit and the end result was likely to be a mess.

'Fasuko,' he turned to look at her again, 'what are you goin' to do now?'

'We are going to the city like I said.' Her eyes lit up, losing a little of their almond-shape just for a fleeting second. She smiled with a bright beauty as if a current of happiness flowed through her. 'The city is wonderful!'

'Yeah? What will ya do there?'

'We will buy a fine house, large and beautiful, with a garden full of flowers. We will have a pony and trap. We will have servants. I will have fine clothes. Everything will be like a new life with the sun shining on us.'

Her features were radiant as if the sun shone from within her. He smiled up at her, something catching in his throat. She was like a pretty child who receives love just for being. He could see her in the garden of flowers, surrounded by beauty which could not compete with her, smiling and laughing at the centre of an admiring throng.

He glanced away, slightly embarrassed for no reason he could figure out. The banks were going past now at an increasing speed as the current picked up. For a moment, his thoughts stayed at Broken Rock, and he saw the corpses lying scattered around, and then the other three back at Humblestream. Somehow it didn't seem to fit too well with Fasuko's vision of the flowered garden. But life had to go on. She was as right about that as she seemed to be about everything else.

He watched her again as she bent to the oar, using it with faultless skill and grace. He had thought to help by taking over the task but he did not believe he could do it well enough. It seemed tricky and he had a horror of turning the boat across the current causing it to capsize, although Fasuko never seemed to have any fear of that happening. He had hardly ever been in a boat before and the whole experience was bringing with it a sense of unreality. He held on to the thwart and looked up at the sky. It was the only thing that seemed to remain unchanging and normal.

After a time, he saw that Fasuko was staring straight ahead with a quiet intensity; he looked to see what she had noticed. The river was fairly rough at this stretch with a strong current, combined with the rising breeze, creating an unruly surface of tiny waves. This was not what Fasuko was looking at. She could obviously handle the boat almost without thinking. What claimed her attention was the ferry, not far ahead, which they must soon reach.

Jerry observed the long, strong rope across the water, stretching from bank to bank, and the buildings on either side, silent and deserted. The sight somehow reinforced the feeling of gloom that he had been trying to fight off, but he had little time to ponder as they drifted swiftly towards the overhanging rope. In a moment they had passed under it, Fasuko bending her head just a little as they did so.

As they went by, Jerry stared at the buildings and the ferry boat itself, safely moored on the east bank. There was nothing to be seen there, except a few chickens and what looked like forgotten washing on a line. When he turned to look at the other bank, he noticed that Fasuko had crouched well down, almost below the level of the gunwale and was steering with her arms held just above her head. She was unable to see exactly where she was going, but she still kept the boat on course.

Surprised, he turned his attention onto the low house to the west of the ferry, and at once noticed a movement.

A man with light, sandy hair stood in a doorway. In his arms, he held a rifle, trained and ready, Jerry ducked to the bottom of the boat as the bullet smashed into its wooden side.

9

Jerry lay at the bottom of the boat while the next bullet flew overhead, singing its way onwards into the river. For some time he did not move, feeling the vulnerability of their situation and hoping they would soon be out of range. Then Fasuko edged herself up, gaining a better grip on the steering oar. She did not look back, her attention taken up by the turbulent water ahead.

'Don't, keep down!' He yelled at her in sudden panic, fearful for her safety. 'You'll get hit!'

'I cannot steer like this. The current is getting too strong. I must stand up to see and steer.'

'Let me do it! Stay down. Come on, let me try.'

'No. You do not know how.'

She stood up, taking command of the tossing craft, steadying it in the fierce current. The rifle crashed again from somewhere far astern but she did not flinch or even glance back at the ferry. It was as if she realized the futility of it. If she was going to be struck down by the next bullet then it would happen. Looking back to where it was coming from could make no difference.

Jerry shook his head in silent admiration for her calm courage and then sat up in order to see how far they had come. To his relief, he saw that the boat was almost out of range of the rifle. Also, the man who had stood in the doorway with the gun had now vanished. Jerry smiled his delight and tried to catch Fasuko's eye but she was looking only straight ahead, no trace of emotion in the delicate beauty of her features.

He stared again at the house by the ferry, half expecting to see a horse and rider appear. For some minutes he could see nothing, but the light swaying of the ferry-line in the rising wind. Then there appeared some dim, unclear faint stir from behind the little jetty. He peered closer, almost certain he could make out the movement of two heads just behind the wooden structure and a blue jacket or dress against the green bank behind. In a moment, however, the figures ducked out of sight to be followed seconds later by a slim, light-coloured shape which eased out from the shadow of the jetty into the stream. He recognized a birch-bark canoe, a long two-seater, strong and as swift as an arrow.

The light craft darted out at an angle across the current and then swung with a quick, graceful movement to face downstream. It did not sway during this dangerous manoeuvre; there was no suggestion that it might overbalance. He saw at once that it was in expert hands.

It advanced in line behind them, almost in the centre of the river and taking full advantage of the strong current. The two paddles dipped in perfect unison propelling the canoe over the surface of the water. Its shallow draught almost allowed it to skim, while the larger, heavier boat had to cut its way through the weight of water as Fasuko threw herself once again into the task of gaining what distance she could.

Jerry's eyes held deep concern as he watched her and the pursuing canoe. It seemed to him that they must soon be overtaken. He lifted the rifle from the thwart and held it ready in his hands.

The figure on the bow of the canoe was the sandy-haired man who had already fired at them. His slim body in its buckskin jacket only partly concealed the blue-dressed bulk of Judy, seated behind, her powerful arms and skilled touch of the paddle urging the slim craft onwards. Their paddles rose and fell in harmony, each uplifting movement catching the sunlight, every dip and thrust shortening the distance.

Jerry studied them in silence, his mind busy. The man in the canoe had a rifle and would use it. Soon he would be close enough to try another shot and provided the light craft could be held steady, there was no reason why he should miss. His target must be Fasuko, standing up in the stern of the boat, with her body and mind focussed on her task.

Fasuko was, he realized, their one disadvantage. She could easily be struck down within the next few minutes. Only if she could somehow keep well down behind the stern-post would she have any chance. With luck the post was thick enough to stop a bullet but she had already said she must stand up to steer on this stretch of water.

Nevertheless, she would have to get down and out of sight as soon as the man raised his rifle. Jerry was determined to make certain that she did. In a few seconds he must warn her, and, if she failed to comply, he would drag her to comparative safety. Somehow, though, he knew she would react quickly and sensibly. She was a determined girl, but she had more sense than to take any unnecessary risk.

He waited, nerves hanging by a thread, ready to act as soon as the man with the sandy hair put down the paddle. At the same time it occurred to him that their pursuers were in as much danger as themselves. The heavy boat in which he was seated made a much firmer platform from which to fire a rifle. Also its sides although by no means bullet-proof, gave better protection than bonded birch-bark. If Fasuko were under cover even for a moment, and they took a chance with the current and reduced speed, his rifle would immediately have the advantage.

He did not doubt that the people in the canoe realized all that too. They must have known even before they launched into the turbulent river that they were taking a great risk.

There was a hint of recklessness in their actions. Perhaps they were enraged at the thought of losing the gold. Gold, he knew by this time, could make people more than a little crazy. But how could they have known the gold was on the boat? He himself had not known until he had jumped aboard, and he could not see how they could have learned of the events at Broken Rock so soon. Perhaps, though, they had found out about the death of young Frank over at Humblestream. Maybe a servant or a farm-hand had ridden over to inform them, and the sudden appearance of the boat had seemed to be their only chance of revenge.

The thought did nothing to make him feel any better about the situation. Frank was just a kid caught up in the mad behaviour of his elders, with little more idea of what was going on than had young Billy, lying dead in the barn. It was all just a crazy mess; one that had not yet finished. He sighed deeply and lifted the rifle, knowing his course of action was inevitable.

He did not have long to wait. The man at the bow of the canoe suddenly dropped his paddle inside and reached down. Jerry yelled out a warning and Fasuko slid behind the stern-post. His own rifle was already pointing into the bow of the canoe, steadied by his arm on the wood. The sandy-haired man had lifted his gun, turning it in his hands. Jerry fired. The bullet seemed to strike the breech of the man's rifle or his hands. He yelled in pain and lurched backwards into Judy. The gun fell from his grasp, bounced on the narrow side of the canoe and dropped into the water. The canoe swung, its two occupants entangled for vital seconds in wild confusion. The man reached out with bloody hands and Judy waved her paddle, striking helplessly. Then it was over and the canoe upturned.

Jerry stared hard, more than half expecting to see their heads appear on the surface. What he would do when that happened he was by no means certain. His gun was still ready but he knew he could not shoot a person struggling in the water.

But there was nothing to be seen except the canoe bobbing along behind the heavier boat, which was beginning to turn as Fasuko lost control. It swung and began to tilt alarmingly but Fasuko knew its broad beam would prevent its capsize. Quickly, however, she pulled herself up and into position. A glance at Jerry's face and then at the upturned canoe informed her the danger was past.

In a moment she had firm grip on the sculling oar and was putting her weight against it, pushing with short, even strokes. Gradually Fasuko straightened the craft so it was in line with the current.

In spite of her skill and speed, the manoeuvre took a few minutes and the canoe, light and half-full of air, almost caught up with them until it was no more than ten yards off. Its curved hull seemed to swim with the rapid current like some partly submerged river creature.

It was then that the arm came from beneath it, fingers outstretched and groping wildly for some means of support.

Jerry sat up, hands on the gunwale, and bent over towards her, willing her to come nearer. He was almost overcome with relief to see that she was still alive but he was also in a frenzy of anxiety lest she should sink from sight. He reached out but she was still much too far away to catch her hand or any part of her clothing.

'Come on, Judy, you can make it!' His words were scarcely audible even to himself for fear and excitement had taken hold of him. He knew she could not hear him, but it seemed that she had seen some movement of his through her water-filled eyes, or she had caught sight of the boat's bulk, for she began to struggle towards it, arms churning in clumsy, awkward strokes, head and shoulders bobbing and sinking with every movement.

Slowly she swam nearer while he leaned further and further over the side, putting himself in danger of falling. Her eyes were on him now, openly imploring and desperately seeking his help. His heart thumped, his arm stretched out for that happy moment when he could grasp her hand so he could begin to pull her to safety.

His hand dipped into the water. His fingers touched hers, curled to grip and fell away. He caught at her wrist but it slipped from him, then he grabbed at her sleeve, clinging to the wet cloth as if to save his own life. His heart swelled as his grip held and she came a few inches nearer. In a moment she was alongside.

'Jerry. Do you . . . should you . . . ?' Fasuko's voice, anxious and strained came from behind him but he had Judy by the shoulders now and was hauling her upwards. He knew he could not get her on board unaided and also realized that Fasuko, even if she dared leave the sculling oar, could only help slightly. For a brief second he despaired but then Judy's strong arms edged their way over the gunwale and suddenly she found the strength to heave herself over. The boat swayed and Jerry dropped to one knee; the old man tottered and almost fell from his seat. Only Fasuko stood steady, hands gripping the heavy oar, bright eyes staring at the vast soaking mass of blue which sprawled on the boards.

Judy's head was bent, her face almost resting on the bottom of the boat, her wild hair covering her forehead. Her breath came in great gasps.

Jerry stared at her, a relieved smile pulling at the corners of his mouth. Thank God she was safe! He had never had anything against Judy. She had always seemed all right to him and had got herself mixed up in this mess through no fault of her own. The fact that she had been intent upon bringing them down with a rifle bullet just minutes before had not turned his mind against her. He believed that he could understand it. Her family had suffered and she must have felt that keenly although it was obvious she could not as yet know the full extent of her loss. Pity and some degree of conscience struggled within him as he looked at her.

Then he saw that she was looking up at him. Her eyes, wild and imploring just a few minutes before, had changed to a dull, smouldering resentment, like those of a baited bear angered to the point of killing.

She glared at Jerry and then her gaze swept beyond him towards Fasuko in the stern. It was then that hatred spread like some swift disease across her features. Her eyes narrowed; her lips curled back in a snarl. Clumsily she got to her feet and her brawny hand groped at her belt. In a moment a wet, glittering knife appeared, gripped tightly in determined fingers. Judy began to move towards the Japanese girl, who stared back at her, face set.

'All thet beauty . . . I'll cut it
. . . from the front of yer head . . . ya
bitch!'

Jerry rose up and launched himself
at her. One hand grasped her by an
arm while the other sought a grip on
her neck. She swayed but refused to
fall. Her left elbow struck him on
the chin. She pulled away from him,
hauling herself over the centre thwart
with a practised ease which belied her
bulk. Then Jerry gained a better footing
and pushed her almost off balance. The
knife swung and he felt the point enter
the wound on his arm. He hissed in
pain but grabbed at her wrist with
both hands so that the shining blade
trembled in the air. They staggered
together across the boat, feet thumping
on the boards while the water seemed
to rise up to meet them.

Then a shadow appeared from
overhead, long and straight, falling
from the sky like some thunderbolt.
The heavy sculling oar missed his
shoulder by a hair's-breadth but then

came a bone-splitting crack as its hard blade smashed into Judy's head and she toppled like some felled tree into the turbulent stream.

'It is not wise to invite the sea-dragon into the golden ship! You are all right, Jerry?'

He stared at her and then nodded in stunned silence.

★ ★ ★

Gradually, the river broadened out and slowed its pace. The sun had shifted to the west and had begun its descent, spilling a red light across the banks and the water. It caught Fasuko's features in a warm glow. Her movements at the oar were easy and relaxed, as if all of time lay ahead of her. She seemed lost in the contemplation of a joyful future, her eyes dreamy and withdrawn, a smile twitching at the corners of her mouth.

Jerry gazed at her with mixed feelings, entranced by her quiet beauty but with some cold, emptiness inside which was not easily filled. After a time, she smiled at him in a way that brought a flickering response.

'Be happy, Jerry,' she said, 'the world can be a wonderful place.'

They were drifting along much nearer the east bank as if she were content to go at the slow pace the river shallows suggested. She began to speak to him with a charming friendliness, for the first time asking about his early life on the farm and around the little town of Bluewater. At first his answers were short and stilted but he slowly overcame his embarrassment at her sudden interest. Finally he relaxed and spoke to her openly and frankly.

After a time, she smiled ruefully and bit her lip, even that little pretence having a charm of its own.

'Jerry, I am sorry, but I must go ashore. I must get off the boat. Just for a little while.'

'Eh, what, why is thet?'

'Oh dear, it is so difficult, so

embarrassing on this boat. I mean, a lady and a man. You see, I must get off. Perhaps it is just all the excitement. So sorry.'

'Yeah, yeah, of course!' He could have kicked himself for being so slow on the uptake. 'Sure.'

He twisted round and saw that she was already steering towards a little peninsula that pushed out from the east bank, sloping and stony but overhung by willow.

'When we get to that place, perhaps you would step ashore with the painter and tie up to the tree, then I can follow.' She smiled again and looked down at her feet as if to hide the shyness in her eyes. 'It might be better if you wait on the boat.'

'Yeah, sure, of course, but this *painter*?'

'The rope at the front of the boat.'

'Hell, of course!'

He stood in the bow, rope in hand, while she steered the craft alongside the pebble beach. When he judged that they were close enough, he swung himself over the side into six inches of water and waded quickly up to the little stretch of dry stones. In a moment, he had crunched his way up the slope to the tree. The willow roots were mostly exposed by years of erosion and it was an easy matter to make the rope secure. He was aware that he was hurrying to oblige her, still annoyed with himself for what he felt had been a lack of consideration for her finer feelings.

'All right, Fasuko, thet should do it!'

He turned around. The rope lay slack on the pebbles, its end bobbing and swinging in the current. The boat was already several yards out and picking up speed under her quick sculling. When she was well out of reach but just before the main current caught her, she straightened and turned to face him, smiling and relaxed.

'I am sorry, Jerry, but I cannot marry a cowboy. I am going to live in the city! I hope you will be happy!'

Something glinted gold in the sun and dropped with a slight metallic sound on the stones at his feet, He did not move as he watched the boat join the main stream. The old man caught sight of him as he stood there on the bank and smiled at him vacantly. Fasuko sculled in her usual smooth manner, head turned from him now, eyes back to the broad river, easing in to the long bend before her.

He was aware of feeling nothing. There was no anger and no disappointment. He was empty, as if he had been scooped out from within.

Slowly the boat shrank in size. The old man vanished from sight. Fasuko became like a little clockwork doll, swaying her arms and shoulders, absorbed in herself.

When the boat reached the bend, she stopped, taking her hands from the oar and fumbled about at her feet. Then she stood up very straight and stared back at him, all the way across that broad stretch of water as if to look carefully into his face. In her hands she held something which glinted faint yellow and it came to him that it was the little brass Buddha. Then she melted into the sunset.

He stared for only a moment longer and then picked up the object she had thrown. It was a coin, broader and heavier than any piece he had ever seen. Confederate gold. He put it into his shirt pocket which was stiff now with hardened blood and turned away.

'I never asked her to marry me,' he protested to himself. 'I never said nothin' about thet at all!'

He climbed up the steep bank, through the tangled willow branches, and began to walk back upstream.

10

By the time he reached the ferry, the sun was well down on the western horizon and the river had fallen into shadow. The buildings on both sides were in gloom and silent. Only the long rope still swayed while the ferry-boat butted sullenly against the jetty. As he walked by he thought of Judy and his mouth tightened as he remembered her sinking under that terrible blow. A chicken flew up from under his feet and startled him. He trudged on, leaving the deserted place behind with the feeling that Judy was somehow still watching his back and whispering to him to look her up next time he came by.

It was a long walk to Broken Rock, but he was hardly aware of his fatigue or the soreness of his feet. It was as if his mind floated on a body that moved mechanically and could not give up even if it wanted to.

The stars shone in glittering display giving enough light to keep him on the narrow track that wound its way along the river-bank. He followed the same route he had taken that other night which had now become just a dim memory. At length, he saw the ground beginning to rise into a low hill to the north. A clump of darker shadow, which was the main building of the farm, stood out against the pale starlight.

Sometime before he could make out the sharp outline of the roof, he saw, lying some distance ahead, a crumpled heap on the track. He stopped, hesitating for a moment, because he knew it was Jed Galbraith lying there, the words of his last accusation silenced in his throat.

He approached slowly, not out of absurd fear, but because he was in the presence of death. Anger and hatred had long deserted him, leaving only a nameless regret.

Jed lay with his face to the earth. In his back, and arm and neck were the deep stab wounds of a bowie knife. Congealed blood had stiffened his clothing. His left hand clawed into the grass. So Casey had given an account of himself and had dragged the life out of Jed Galbraith.

He bent over the body but did not touch it for it seemed that there was nothing he could do. The bloody battle had run its course and he had survived to think on it, to make sense of it if he could. He was straightening himself up when he saw a movement. The slightest of tremors ran through Jed's body and the faintest sound of breath came — a hiss into the ground beneath his mouth.

Jerry froze for a second, his feelings in disarray but then he took the man by one shoulder and eased him up a little, turning his face out of the dirt. To roll him on to his wounded back, would, he reasoned, be a bad idea. For the bleeding seemed to have ceased but could well begin again if the clotted blood was disturbed.

Jed was still breathing, not regularly but in occasional gasps. It seemed that Jerry had no chance of saving him, but even an outside possibility could not be ignored.

He ran to the house and found water and some cloth and returned quickly. He pressed the dampened rag to the forehead of the wounded man and watched anxiously as the eyes flickered open. In those few minutes, crouching there in the lonely night, it seemed to him that this man's life was of all-consuming importance.

Why? The question leapt into his mind. Why should he care about this man who had sought to kill him and who would have done so if things had worked out differently? Even if, by some strange twist of fate, Jerry had been able to lead him to the gold, he would have repaid the kindness with a bullet rather than allow his guilty secret to find its way, by whatever devious route, back to his own family. That much Jerry had known from the moment Jed had made the offer of sharing the treasure between them. The gold, if it had ever been found, would have gone with Jed Galbraith into some unknown future. Jerry would have taken a bullet as soon as he was of no further use.

Why then? Why try to save this killer who had shown no trace of mercy in anything he had said or done?

He knew the answer well enough. It was because the man was wounded, helpless and dying. There was not enough hate left in him to walk away.

Only slowly did Jed regain full consciousness. His breathing became a little easier and his lips moved as if to speak. Jerry helped him to drink, holding him steady as he began to writhe in his pain.

'Easy. Don't move. You gotta stay still.'

'You. It's you! The Reb!' The voice

came rasping, full of hate and pain. 'You murdered my father!'

Jerry shook his head. The words struck him hard. Senseless as they were, he felt he must deny this accusation which the man seemed to have carried into death and back.

'No. You got it wrong. We fought and he came off worst. Thet was it. He was goin' to kill the gal and me too. It was no murder. Think on it. You'll see thet, if you think a little.'

'An' me too. Look what ya did to me.'

'It was Casey. You fought him, remember?'

'But you hit me. You hurt me bad.'

Jerry looked at the ugly, distorted mouth and remembered how the sharp, upward blow of his own head had further damaged it. The pain must have been very great. It was all hell! The whole thing was hell!

'I had to save the gal. They were goin' to kill her.'

Jed lay still again, seeming to brood

deep within himself, then he gave a twisted rueful grin that brought with it another grimace of pain.

'Pa was allus a hard man, hard on us all when we was young. I'd have took thet gold myself if I could.' He dropped again into silence, then he whispered: 'The Chinee gal. She went off with the gold, thet right? Crafty bitch!' He groaned suddenly in renewed pain. 'God, oh God!'

His throat was beginning to heave. His torn mouth twisted open and hung slack. Jerry looked deep into his eyes. It was like looking into a dark ravine with no bottom. He pressed a little more water to the drooping lips.

'You're not a bad kinda feller, Reb . . . damned war sent everybody crazy as hell.'

There was silence but for the night wind.

Jerry lowered the man's head to the ground and then stood up. He wondered if it had been worthwhile. Was there any sense in extending a dying man's life for a little longer, if that, in fact, was what he had done? Had there been any point in the water, the hand under the shoulders, the few kindly words? Would it have been any worse if Jed had simply died alone in the night? Somehow, he thought it would have been, for the dark hatred would still have been there.

He went over to the shed near the rocks and rummaged around inside until he found what had caught his eye when he had crept past before, rifle in hand, to take on Henry. It was a saddle and saddlebag, old and worn — an army saddle — almost certainly that of Cousin Coney. He fitted it carefully to his own horse and then led it around to the jetty. On his way, he noticed the mule, still tethered, and he stopped to set it free to fend for itself. On the jetty, he caught the glint of gold in the moonlight and picked up some coins which had obviously fallen from a bag in the haste to load the boat while Jed careered towards them. He peered at them in the moonlight, felt the unworn surface of each and then let them drop to the ground.

He then mounted up and turned downriver.

She was waiting for him at the ferry. He saw her slight figure standing very still and casting a long shadow in the moonlight. He caught sight of her from some distance and he guessed she had not moved for a long time but had been listening to the sounds of his approaching horse carrying through the still night air.

When he was up close she took a step forward and looked up at him. The pale light further enhanced her beauty and her eyes seemed to shine with a brilliance that made him gasp. She did not smile. There was an air of tension about her as if she waited to hear his first word, to see if it would make her turn aside into the shadows and vanish like a nervous fawn.

'Fasuko. How is it thet you're here?' He sounded surprised and made no

174

attempt to disguise the delight that he felt on seeing her. 'I thought you had gone way down the river.'

For a brief moment she did not reply then she said, 'I did Jerry . . . way down the river. Then I did not feel so good. It was as if I was going nowhere.'

'What about the city?'

'The city. Yes, the city.' She smiled now and then looked away. 'Well, the city did not seem so good. It fell down before I saw it, like in an earthquake. It did not seem to matter any more but I went on steering the boat until my father looked up at me — and into me — and said, 'Where is the young man with the kind eyes?' After that I steered into the bank and tied up safely, made sure my father was comfortable and then I walked all the way back. I thought you would go to Broken Rock for your horse and then would try to cross by the ferry. I wanted to see you first.'

Jerry could say nothing. He stared

at her, his heart beginning to thump harder than it had during his fight with the Galbraiths.

'I know I was wrong to trick you like that, Jerry, to leave you standing at the side of the river as if you did not matter.'

'Thet's all right, it don't matter.'

'Do you forgive me?'

'Sure, what the . . . I mean, I never . . . ' His voice trailed off in embarrassment.

'I did not come all the way back just to ask forgiveness.' She was staring up at him now, her lips curling in a smile. 'What I said about not wanting to marry you . . . that was not right.'

'That don't matter either. I never asked you anyhow.'

'Oh.' She kicked a little stone aside with the toe of her dusty boot. 'No. Well, I thought . . . About all that gold, Jerry, we can share it.'

'Yeah?' He smiled and laughed for the first time with a slightly sardonic edge to his voice, then he paused and went on kindly, 'Thet gold, Fasuko, is all Confederate. Good, solid stuff in its time but you kin never buy anything with it without all kinds of questions being asked about where it came from. The only way would be to melt it down and get what you can for it thet way. But thet means dealing with criminals Fasuko, and you've seen enough of those kind of men to last you the rest of your life.'

'I know.' She looked at the trail as if needing time for his words to sink in. 'All that should have mattered was getting my father safely out of that animals' den. The gold should not have mattered. Only it started to drive me crazy.'

'Like it did everybody, Fasuko.'

'Except you.'

'Well, even I liked the look of it at first.'

They suddenly smiled at one another, openly and frankly, and laughed together.

'Thing is Fasuko, I've got a good enough little farm down at Bluewater.

It's a mite neglected but all it really needs is a couple of people to put in a long stretch of hard work and it'll be jest dandy! So what about you gittin' up behind me on this horse and we'll ride back to Broken Rock slow and easy? Then we'll hitch up the mule to the wagon and move downriver to pick up your pa. At the next ford we can cross over and head for thet swell little farm. What do ya say?'

For the first time ever, he saw her momentarily lost for words, then she laughed loudly, pleased and excited.

'That sounds, like you say, Jerry, fine and dandy! But I will not come as your servant!'

'Well, I guess I jest might change my mind about not asking you to marry me.'

He reached down to grasp her slight fingers and drew her up behind him. In a moment her arms were around his waist and her head was buried in the small of his back and he felt that he had enough of gold to last for all time.

Other titles in the Linford Western Library

THE CROOKED SHERIFF
John Dyson

Black Pete Bowen quit Texas with a burning hatred of men who try to take the law into their own hands. But he discovers that things aren't much different in the silver mountains of Arizona.

THEY'LL HANG BILLY FOR SURE:
Larry & Stretch
Marshall Grover

Billy Reese, the West's most notorious desperado, was to stand trial. From all compass points came the curious and the greedy, the riff-raff of the frontier. Suddenly, a crazed killer was on the loose — but the Texas Trouble-Shooters were there, girding their loins for action.

RIDERS OF RIFLE RANGE
Wade Hamilton

Veterinarian Jeff Jones did not like open warfare — but it was there on Scrub Pine grass. When he diagnosed a sick bull on the Endicott ranch as having the contagious blackleg disease, he got involved in the warfare — whether he liked it or not!

BEAR PAW
Nevada Carter

Austin Dailey traded two cows to a pair of Indians for a bay horse, which subsequently disappeared. Tracks led to a secret hideout of fugitive Indians — and cattle thieves. Indians and stockmen co-operated against the rustlers. But it was Pale Woman who acted as interpreter between her people and the rangemen.

THE WEST WITCH
Lance Howard

Detective Quinton Hilcrest journeys west, seeking the Black Hood Bandits' lost fortune. Within hours of arriving in Hags Bend, he is fighting for his life, ensnared with a beautiful outcast the town claims is a witch! Can he save the young woman from the angry mob?

GUNS OF THE PONY EXPRESS
T. M. Dolan

Rich Zennor joined the Pony Express venture at the start, as second-in-command to tough Denning Hartman. But Zennor had the problems of Hartman believing that they had crossed trails in the past, and the fact that he was strongly attached to Hartman's Indian girl, Conchita.

BLACK JO OF THE PECOS
Jeff Blaine

Nobody knew where Black Josephine Callard came from or whither she returned. Deputy U.S. Marshal Frank Haggard would have to exercise all his cunning and ability to stay alive before he could defeat her highly successful gang and solve the mystery.

RIDE FOR YOUR LIFE
Johnny Mack Bride

They rode west, hoping for a new start. Then they met another broken-down casualty of war, and he had a plan that might deliver them from despair. But the only men who would attempt it would be the truly brave — or the desperate. They were both.

THE NIGHTHAWK
Charles Burnham

While John Baxter sat looking at the ruin that arsonists had made of his log house, a stranger rode into the yard. Baxter and Walt Showalter partnered up and re-built the house. But when it was dynamited, they struck back — and all hell broke loose.

MAVERICK PREACHER
M. Duggan

Clay Purnell was hopeful that his posting to Capra would be peaceable enough. However, on his very first day in town he rode into trouble. Although loath to use his .45, Clay found he had little choice — and his likeness to a notorious bank robber didn't help either!

SIXGUN SHOWDOWN
Art Flynn

After years as a lawman elsewhere, Dan Herrick returned to his old Arizona stamping ground to find that nesters were being driven from their homesteads by ruthless ranchers. Before putting away his gun once and for all, Dan forced a bloody and decisive showdown.

RIDE LIKE THE DEVIL!
Sam Gort

Ben Trunch arrived back on the Big T only to find that land-grabbing was in progress. He confronted Luke Fletcher, saloon-keeper and town boss, with what was happening, and was immediately forced to ride for his life. But he got the chance to put it all right in the end.

SLOW WOLF AND DAN FOX:
Larry & Stretch
Marshall Grover

The deck was stacked against an innocent man. Larry Valentine played detective, and his investigation propelled the Texas Trouble-Shooters into a gun-blazing fight to the finish.

BRANAGAN'S LAW
Alan Irwin

To Angus Flint, the valley was his domain and he didn't want any new settlers. But Texas Ranger Jim Branagan had other ideas. Could he put an end to Flint's tyranny for good?

THE DEVIL RODE A PINTO
Bret Rey

When a settler is cut to ribbons in a frenzied attack, Texas Ranger Sam Buck learns that the killer is Rufus Berry, known as The Devil. Sam stiffens his resolve to kill or capture Berry and break up his gang.

THE DEATH MAN
Lee F. Gregson

The hardest of men went in fear of Ford, the bounty hunter, who had earned the name 'The Death Man'. Yet even Ford was not infallible — when he killed the wrong man, he found that he was being sought himself by the feared Frank Ambler.

LEAD LANGUAGE
Gene Tuttle

After Blaze Colton and Ricky Rawlings have delivered a train load of cows from Arizona to San Francisco, they become involved in a load of trouble and find themselves on the run!

A DOLLAR FROM THE STAGE
Bill Morrison

Young saddle-tramp Len Finch stumbled into a web of murder, lawlessness, intrigue and evil ambition. In the end, he put his life on the line for the folks that he cared about.